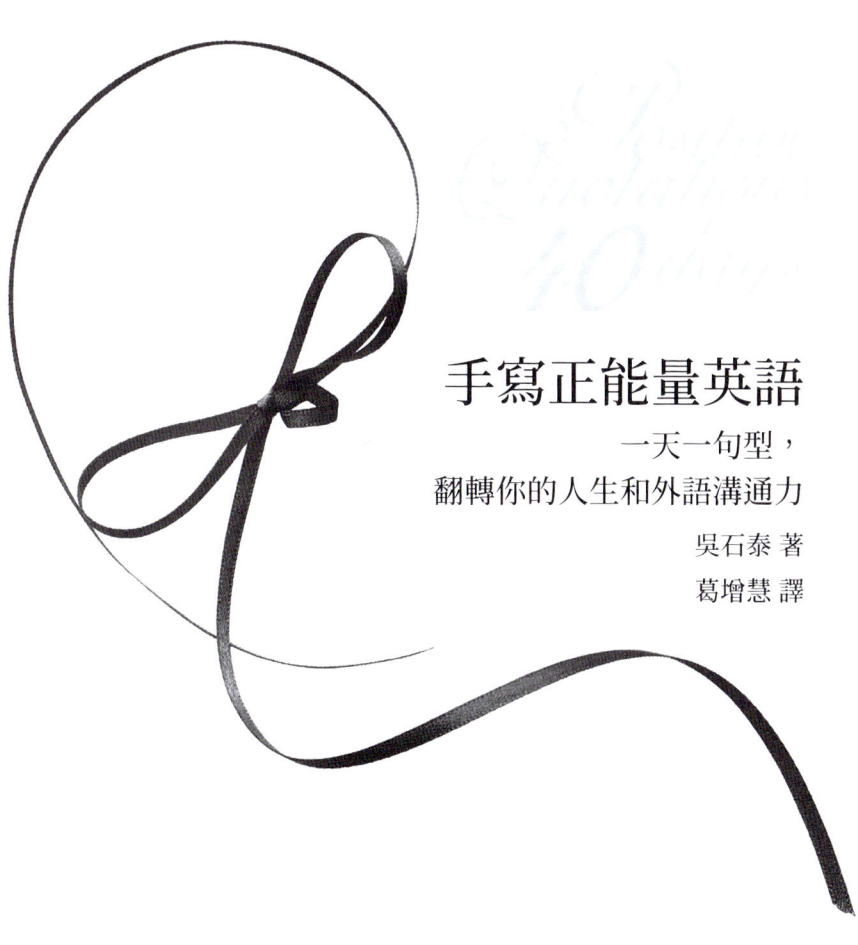

手寫正能量英語

一天一句型，
翻轉你的人生和外語溝通力

吳石泰 著

葛增慧 譯

前言

　　這個世界並非總是充滿正能量，相反的，世界充斥著許多阻礙正能量的病毒。然而，正向思考的影響力無窮，只要一絲正能量，就能瞬間瓦解周遭的負面病毒。人就是這樣的生命體，因此，將心態調整為正向模式至關重要。

　　在國際化的現代，英語是全球最通行的語言。為了學好英語，我們付出了各種代價。不論年齡，許多人總是圍繞著基礎英文打轉。在對「基礎」一知半解的情況下，卻盲目地套用各種不適合自己的基礎學習法。

　　何不以正面心態來學習英語呢？找到適合自己年齡、個性、語文程度的英語，才是學習的最佳起點。同樣的，適合自己年齡、個性、能力程度的正向思考，才是培養正面心態的起點。

　　帶著這樣的期望，我寫下了這本書，讓讀者能透過抄寫正能量的句子來學習基礎英語。

現在，讓我們來開始為期 40 天的英文正能量訓練。但請不要躁進，也請不要強迫自己完成所有的訓練量。根據自己身體和心理的情況，合理安排每天的訓練量。即使反覆看同一天的內容也無妨，甚至可以把一天的內容練習一整週。但請千萬不要放棄。放棄就等於放棄了積極的人生，也等於把好不容易找到的合適英語教材給撕碎了。

世界是圍繞著準備好的人運轉的。準備沒有固定的模式，你需要用自己的方式去做。讓自己轉換成正能量模式，找到適合自己的英語學習法，這小小的轉變將成為你未來堅實的基礎。站起來，穩住腳步！你會發現，曾經讓你感到不安的立足點，已經變成你最可靠的支撐。世界的大門，必為你敞開。

本書使用方法

本書是一個爲期 8 週的正能量英語抄寫練習，
請在週一到週五，每天投資 10 分鐘。
書裡所有英文語句都有 MP3 朗讀音檔，可以掃描下方 QR code 邊聽邊練習。

STEP 1
today's quotation
今天的正能量英語佳句。

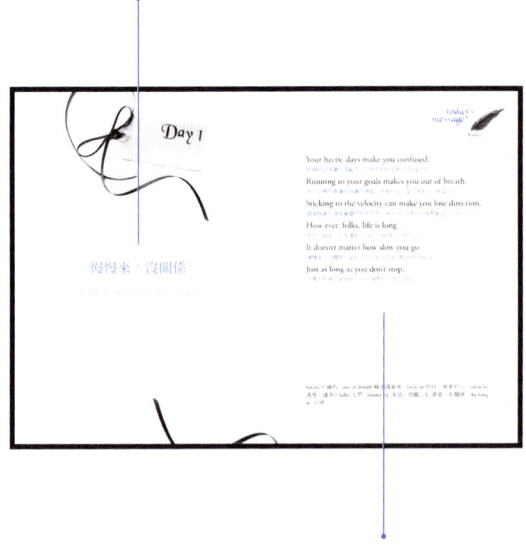

STEP 2
today's message
請播放 MP3 朗誦音檔，
一句一句跟著唸
爲自己帶來正能量的英語。

STEP 3
抄寫
在指定頁面邊寫邊大聲跟著唸。

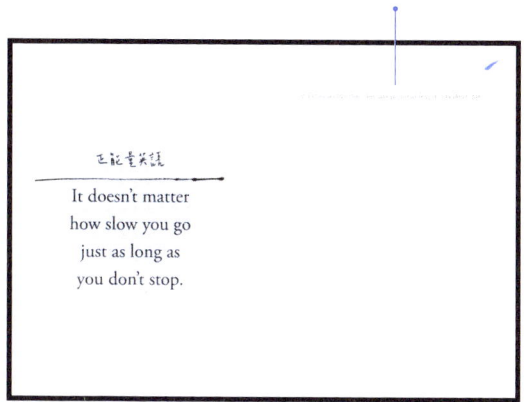

STEP 4
句型
為期 8 週,每天都有一個句型,
總共可以學到 40 個句型。
記得邊聽邊跟讀。

STEP 6
抄寫與句型熟練
一邊抄寫完整的句型和對話,
一邊跟讀讓自己熟練,
最後,寫下自己的造句來進行應用。

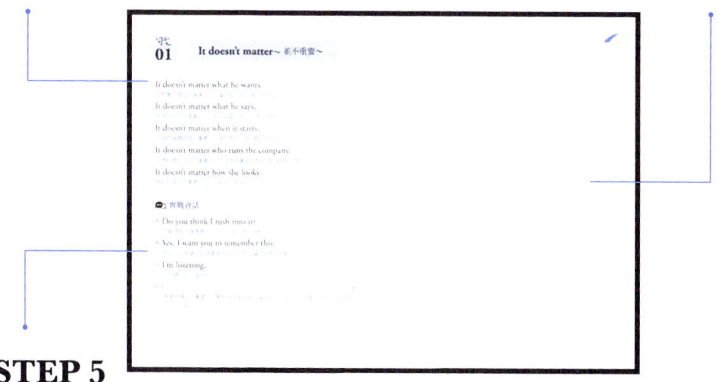

STEP 5
實戰會話
透過會話練習,深刻理解句型應用方式,以此培養英文語感。
請在空白欄位進行造句以利複習。

contents

前言　002
本書使用方法　004

1 week　每天都是初心

- Day 1　慢慢來，沒關係　句型1 It doesn't matter ~　012
- Day 2　為了擺脫困境，你必須經歷它　句型2 You must ~　018
- Day 3　你可以做任何事，但不是所有事　句型3 You can ~　024
- Day 4　如同不需要錢一樣工作，如同從未受過傷一樣去愛　句型4 like　030
- Day 5　即使在正確的路上，你仍須繼續前進　句型5 Even if　036

2 week　人生解藥

- Day 6　好奇心是無聊的解藥　句型6 cure for　044
- Day 7　行善心安，作惡不安　句型7 When I ~　050
- Day 8　瘋狂就是不斷重複同樣的事情　句型8 over and over　056
- Day 9　成功只有一種，就是你能夠用自己的方式過一生　句型9 There is ~　062
- Day 10　放下吧！　句型10 I heard somebody + v.　068

3 week　愛讓我們再次相信

- Day 11　療癒來自於承擔責任　句型 11　come from　076
- Day 12　善於傾聽的人不僅受人歡迎，還能增廣見聞　句型 12　after a while　082
- Day 13　為了理解而傾聽　句型 13　listen to　088
- Day 14　信任是會感染的，不信任也會　句型 14　lack of　094
- Day 15　善心永不落空　句型 15　Don't fail to　100

4 week　一切都會過去

- Day 16　所有的逆境都有機會　句型 16　in the middle of ~　108
- Day 17　挫敗只是一時的　句型 17　make A + adj.　114
- Day 18　只要堅持夠久，我們就能做到任何想做的事　句型 18　as long as　120
- Day 19　每次歷經逆境，我們都會被精煉如黃金　句型 19　this way　126
- Day 20　持之以恆，你會戰勝任何情況　句型 20　more　132

5 week　活出自己的價值

Day 21　每個人都應該立下目標去達成　句型 21 lie in　140
Day 22　如果想要不曾擁有過的東西，就要做不曾做過的事
　　　　句型 22 You've never + p.p.　146
Day 23　擁有好點子的最佳方式，就是產生大量的點子　句型 23 used to ~　152
Day 24　想要活出創意人生，就不要害怕犯錯　句型 24 You must have + p.p.　158
Day 25　你今日的夢想將會創造你的未來　句型 25 Are you sure ~?　164

6 week　現在，就幸福

Day 26　所有的時間都是相連的，過去、現在及未來　句型 26 ahead of　172
Day 27　如果想要幸福，請放下過去　句型 27 prevent A from B　178
Day 28　原諒不能改變過去，但是可以擴展未來　句型 28 difference　184
Day 29　生命不在於長度，而在於深度　句型 29 Have you ~?　190
Day 30　知足常樂　句型 30 happy with　196

7 week 肯定自己

Day 51 你出生的那一天，就被賦予了創造自己的力量 句型 31 I feel ~ 204
Day 52 通往成功的重要關鍵是自信。而自信的重要關鍵在於準備 句型 32 key to 210
Day 53 當你說你做得到，你就釋出了內在創造力 句型 33 I can't ~ 216
Day 54 贏得勝利的人，是那些覺得自己做得到的人 句型 34 Those who ~ 222
Day 55 失敗是可以重新學習的機會 句型 35 afraid of 228

8 week 準備好的幸運

Day 56 成功是站在失敗的肩膀上 句型 36 don't have to 236
Day 57 機會總是會來。打開門迎接機會吧！ 句型 37 You have to ~ 242
Day 58 名聲是煙霧，人氣是偶然，唯一能持續的只有品性 句型 38 endure 248
Day 59 不要害怕受傷 句型 39 It means ~ 254
Day 60 樂在其中就會帶來成功 句型 40 lead to 260

實戰會話解答

1 week

每天都是初心

慢慢來，沒關係

It doesn't matter how slow you go.

Your hectic days make you confused.
忙碌的日子讓你混亂不已。하루하루, 바쁘고 정신없지요.

Running to your goals makes you out of breath.
為了目標狂奔讓你快喘不過氣。목표만 보고 달리면 숨이 가빠집니다.

Sticking to the velocity can make you lose direction.
過度執著於速度會讓你失去方向。속도에만 집착하면 방향을 잃기도 하고요.

How ever, folks, life is long.
然而,朋友,人生漫長。그러나 여러분, 인생은 깁니다.

It doesn't matter how slow you go.
慢慢來,沒關係。얼마나 느리게 가는지는 중요하지 않아요.

Just as long as you don't stop.
只要你別停下來就好。단지, 멈추지만 않는다면요.

hectic 忙碌的 | out of breath 喘不過氣來 | stick to 堅持、執著於～ | velocity 速度、速率 | folks 人們 | matter n. 事情、問題;v. 重要、有關係 | As long as 只要

正能量英語

It doesn't matter
how slow you go
just as long as
you don't stop.

It doesn't matter how slow you go just as long as you don't stop.

句型 01 It doesn't matter~ 並不重要~

It doesn't matter what he wants.
他想要什麼並不重要。그가 뭘 원하든 그건 중요하지 않아.

It doesn't matter what he says.
他說什麼並不重要。그가 무슨 말을 하든 그건 중요하지 않아.

It doesn't matter when it starts.
什麼時候開始並不重要。언제 시작하느냐는 중요하지 않아.

It doesn't matter who runs the company.
由誰經營公司並不重要。누가 그 회사를 운영하는지는 중요하지 않아.

It doesn't matter how she looks.
她的外貌並不重要。그녀의 외모는 중요하지 않아.

💬 實戰會話

A: Do you think I rush into it?
你覺得我太躁進嗎？내가 그 일을 너무 서두르는 것 같아?

B: Yes. I want you to remember this.
是的。我希望你記得這個。그래. 네가 이걸 기억했으면 좋겠어.

A: I'm listening.
我在聽。뭔데, 말해봐.

B: (   )
速度多慢並不重要，只要別停下來就好。얼마나 느리게 가느냐는 중요하지 않아. 멈추지만 않는다면.

為了擺脫困境，
你必須經歷它

To get out of difficulty, you must go through it.

You had a hard time today.
你度過了辛苦的一天。오늘 참 힘든 하루였죠.

You call your friend to have a drink with him/her.
你打電話給朋友想要跟他/她喝一杯。친구에게 전화해서 술 한 잔 하자고 합니다.

You want to drink your hard time off.
你想借酒澆愁。술과 함께 힘든 마음에서 벗어나려고요.

But you find yourself back on the same track in the morning.
但是早上醒來,你發現自己又回到原來的狀態。그런데 아침이 되면 다시 원상태에요.

You want to get out of difficulty.
你想要擺脫困境。힘든 일에서 벗어나고 싶죠.

Then, go through it and beat it.
那就去面對它,迎戰它。그러면, 부딪혀야죠. 부딪혀서 이겨내야죠.

To get out of difficulty, you must go through it.
為了擺脫困境,你必須經歷它。어려움에서 벗어나려면, 반드시 그것을 통과해야 해요.

---

to get out of 逃避、擺脫 | difficulty 困境(形容詞為 difficult)| go through 經歷、遭受、走過

正能量英語

To get out of difficulty, you must go through it.

To get out of difficulty, you must go through it.

句型 02　You must~ 你必須~

You must go through difficulty.
你必須經歷困難。너는 어려움을 반드시 겪어봐야 돼.

You must listen to her.
你必須聽她的。너는 그녀의 말을 반드시 들어야 돼.

You must pass the test.
你必須通過考試。너는 그 시험을 반드시 통과해야 돼.

You must follow the regulations.
你必須遵守規定。너는 그 규칙들을 반드시 지켜야 해.

You must hand in the report by tomorrow.
你必須在明天之前提交報告。너는 그 보고서를 내일까지 반드시 제출해야 돼.

💬 實戰會話

A: What's up?
怎麼了？오늘 어땠어?

B: I had a hard time today.
我今天不太順。정말 힘든 하루였어.

A: How about drinking it off?
喝一杯然後讓它過去好嗎？한 잔 하고 털어버릴까?

B: Sounds good.
聽起來不錯。좋아.

A: (　　　　　　　　　　　　　　　　　　　　　)
為了擺脫困境，你必須經歷它。어려움에서 벗어나려면 반드시 그것을 통과해야 해.

你可以做任何事，
但不是所有事

You can do anything, but not everything.

today's message

What should I do?"
「我該怎麼做？」 "무엇을 해야 할까?"

"What should I do for a living?"
「我該如何維生？」 "무엇으로 먹고 살아야 할까?"

You can see no future ahead of you.
你可能看不到未來。당신 앞의 미래가 보이지 않지요.

However, you should be proud of yourself.
然而，你應以自己為榮。하지만 그럴수록 자신감을 가져야 하죠.

You can do anything.
你可以做任何事。무엇이든 할 수 있어요.

You can't do everything, though.
但你無法做所有事。그래도 모든 걸 할 수는 없죠.

Make up your mind and stick to it.
下定決心，並堅持下去。마음의 결정을 내리고 굳세게 밀어붙이세요.

You can be the top in your field.
你可以在你的領域裡成為佼佼者。그 분야에서 최고가 될 수 있어요.

be proud of oneself 以某人為榮 | make up one's mind 下定決心 | stick to 執著於

正能量英語

You can do anything,
but not everything.

You can do anything, but not everything.

句型 03　You can~ 你可以~

You can get there on time.
你可以準時抵達那裡。넌 제시간에 그곳에 도착할 수 있겠어.

You can find the solution.
你可以找到解決方案。넌 해결책을 찾아낼 수 있을 거야.

You can keep doing it.
你可以持續做。그렇게 계속하면 돼.

You can meet him there.
你可以在那裡見到他。넌 거기에서 그를 만날 수 있어.

You can solve the problem on your own.
你可以自己解決這個問題。그건 너 혼자 해결할 수 있는 문제야.

💬 實戰會話

A: Do you think I can do it?
你覺得我做得到嗎？내가 그걸 할 수 있다고 생각해?

B: Yes. You can do it.
當然。你做得到。그럼. 넌 할 수 있어.

A: Are you sure?
你確定嗎？확신해?

B: Positive. （　　　　　　　　　　　　　　　　）
當然。你可以做任何事。당연하지. 넌 무슨 일이든 할 수 있어.

A: But not everything.
但不是所有事。하지만 모든 걸 할 수 있는 건 아니잖아.

如同不需要錢一樣工作，
如同從未受過傷一樣去愛

Work like you don't need money,
love like you've never been hurt.

Don't go after money.
不要追逐金錢。돈을 쫓지 마세요.

Going after money prevents you from concentrating on work heartily.
追逐金錢會讓你無法專心工作。돈을 쫓으면 일에 제대로 몰두할 수 없어요.

Going after money makes you just try to get the knack of making money.
追逐金錢讓你變得只會掌握賺錢的技巧。돈을 쫓으면 돈 버는 요령만 알게 될 뿐이에요.

Work like you don't need money.
要如同你不需要錢一樣的工作。일하세요, 돈이 필요 없는 것처럼.

Don't let your broken heart show.
不要表現出你的難過。마음의 아픔을 드러내지 마세요.

New love can be a real one.
新萌芽的戀情也有可能是真愛。새로 찾아온 사랑이 진정한 사랑일지 몰라요.

A broken heart shouldn't push your new love away.
不該因為傷心而推開新的戀情。새로운 사랑을 과거의 상처로 밀어내지 마세요.

Love like you've never been hurt.
要如同你不曾受過傷一樣的去愛。사랑하세요, 한 번도 상처받지 않은 것처럼.

---

have never been 不曾 | go after 追逐 | prevent A from B 阻止 A 做 B | concentrate on 專注於 | heartily 衷心的、誠摯的 | get the knack of 獲得訣竅 | broken heart 心碎

正能量英語

Work like you don't need money, love like you've never been hurt.

Work like you don't need money, love like you've never been hurt.

句型 04　like 像~（一樣）

She looks like you.
她長得像你。그녀는 널 닮았어.

I used to be exactly like you.
我也曾經像你一樣。나도 한때는 꼭 너 같았어.

Just do like I said.
就照著我說的做。그냥 내가 말한 것처럼 해.

I like soccer like you do.
我像你一樣喜歡足球。나도 너처럼 축구 좋아해.

I'm into playing computer games like you are.
我像你一樣沉迷電腦遊戲。나도 너처럼 컴퓨터 게임에 빠져 있어.

💬 實戰會話

A: (　　　　　　　　　　　　　　　　　　　　　　)
如同不曾受過傷一樣的去愛！사랑하라고. 한 번도 상처받지 않은 것처럼.

B: What?
什麼？뭐?

A: New love can be a real one.
新的戀情也有可能是真愛啊！새로운 사랑이 진짜 사랑일 수 있어.

B: Come on.
說什麼啦！왜 그러니.

Day 5

即使在正確的路上，
你仍須繼續前進

Even if you're on the right track,
you have to keep moving on.

today's message

You're on the right track.
你走在正確的道路上。옳은 길로 들어섰군요.

You set your goals right.
你設定了正確的目標。목표도 제대로 잡았고요.

You, however, don't just sit there.
然而,你不能就坐在那裡。그렇다고 그대로 앉아 있진 마세요.

You'll get run over, then.
到時,你將會被超越。그러다가 지나가는 차에 치일 거예요.

Don't allow yourself to fall into mannerism.
別讓自己陷在習性裡。매너리즘에 빠지지 마세요.

You're going to die out, then.
到時,你就會被淘汰。그러면 순식간에 도태되니까요.

Move on.
前進。움직이세요.

Don't stop moving.
不要停止前進。멈추지 말고 움직이세요.

---

be on the right track (為了達成目標)進入對的軌道 | set one's goals right 訂立目標 | get run over 被超越,被碾過 | allow oneself to 允許某人(做) | mannerism 習性 | die out 逐漸消失、被淘汰 | move on 往前走

正能量英語

Even if you're on the right track, you have to keep moving on.

Even if you're on the right track, you have to keep moving on.

句型 05　even if　即使（縱使）

Even if it hurts me, I won't give up.
縱使會受傷，我也不會放棄。상처받더라도, 포기하지 않겠어.

Even if you're right, they won't agree with you.
就算你是對的，他們也不會同意你。네가 옳다 해도, 그들은 절대 너에게 동의하지 않을 거야.

Even if she doesn't love me, I'll stay with her.
縱使她不愛我，我也會和她在一起。그녀가 나를 사랑하지 않아도, 나는 그녀와 함께 있을 거야.

Even if you work hard, you won't get promoted.
即使努力工作，你也不會獲得升遷。네가 열심히 일해도, 승진하지는 않을 거야.

Even if you pay me a lot, I can't meet the deadline.
就算你付再多錢，我也無法趕上截止時間。내게 돈을 아무리 많이 줘도, 마감시간에 맞출 수 없어.

💬 實戰會話

A: Am I doing all right?
我做得還可以嗎？저 잘하고 있는 거예요?

B: Yes, you are. (　　　　)
沒錯。你在對的路上。그래. 제대로 잘하고 있어.

A: Am I? I'm happy to hear that.
是嗎？很開心聽到你這樣說。그래요? 그 말을 들으니 정말 다행이에요.

B: But you shouldn't fall into mannerism.
但你不應該陷入慣性。하지만 매너리즘에 빠지면 안 돼.

A: I'll keep that in mind.
我會銘記在心。명심할게요.

Positive Quotations 40 days

2 week

人生解藥

Day 6

好奇心是無聊的解藥

The cure for boredom is curiosity.

today's message

Things must be boring.
事情肯定無聊。따분하지요.

Your daily routine can be boring.
你日常例行的工作可能很無聊。다람쥐 쳇바퀴 돌 듯 뻔한 일상이 지루하지요.

It can happen to everyone.
任何人都是一樣的。누구나 그럴 수 있어요.

How about expanding the range of your interests?
不如擴展你的興趣範圍？관심사의 범위를 넓히는 건 어떨까요?

You trigger your intellectual curiosity.
你驅動自己的求知欲。지적 호기심을 발휘해 봐요.

Then you can chase away boredom.
你就可以驅散無聊。그러면 권태를 없앨 수 있답니다.

The cure for boredom is curiosity.
好奇心是無聊的解藥。지루함에 가장 좋은 치료법은 호기심이에요.

boredom 枯燥，無聊 | boring 無聊的 | expand 拓展，擴張 | range of ～的範圍 | trigger 驅動；（槍砲的）觸發器，導火線 | chase away 驅逐 | curiosity 好奇心

正能量英語

The cure for boredom is curiosity.

The cure for boredom is curiosity.

06 cure for 為～的對策 / 治療方法

There's no cure for AIDS.
愛滋病是沒有解藥的。에이즈 치료법은 없어.

There's no easy cure for alcoholism.
酒精上癮並無簡單的治療方法。알콜 중독에 쉬운 치료법은 없어.

There was no known cure for that.
沒有已知的治療方法。그것에 대한 치료법은 알려져 있지 않았어.

We should find a cure for that.
我們應該找出治療方法。우리는 그것에 대한 대책을 찾아야 해.

What's the cure for that?
治療方法是什麼？그 일에 대한 대책이 뭐야?

💬 實戰會話

A: My daily routine, it is really boring.
我的日常例行工作，真的很枯燥。반복되는 평범한 일상, 정말 따분해.

B: I understand. Why don't you expand the range of your interests?
我懂。你何不拓展你的興趣範圍？이해해. 관심사의 범위를 넓혀 보면 어때?

A: The range of my interests? How?
我的興趣範圍嗎？怎麼拓展？관심사의 범위? 어떻게?

B: ( ) Just trigger your intellectual curiosity.
無聊的解藥是好奇心。你就驅動自己的求知慾吧！지루함의 치료약은 호기심이야. 지적 호기심을 자극해 봐.

Day 7

行善心安；
作惡不安

When I do good, I feel good;
when I do bad, I feel bad.

today's message

Do you feel good today?
你今天心情好嗎？오늘 하루 기분이 좋으셨나요?

You must have done something good.
你一定是做了什麼好事。무언가 좋은 일을 하셨군요.

Do you feel bad today?
你今天心情不好嗎？오늘 하루 기분이 나쁘셨나요?

You must have done something bad.
你一定做了什麼壞事。무언가 나쁜 일을 하셨군요.

You should do something good, even a small thing.
你應該做些好事，縱使那是一件小事。사소한 일이라도 좋은 일을 해야 합니다.

You should not do anything bad, even a little thing.
你不應該做任何壞事，縱使是一件小事。사소한 일이라도 나쁜 일은 하지 않아야 합니다.

That is my religion.
這是我的信仰。그것이 나의 종교입니다.

feel good 心情好 | must have+p.p. 肯定是 | should 應該做 | religion 宗教信仰，狂熱的愛好

正能量英語

When I do good,
I feel good;
when I do bad,
I feel bad.

When I do good, I feel good; when I do bad, I feel bad.

句型 07　When I~ 當我~

When I start the engine, the radio comes on.
當我發動引擎，收音機就會開啟。(차에) 시동을 걸면, 라디오가 나와.

When I was in college, I imagined traveling around Europe.
讀大學的時候，我夢想去歐洲四處旅遊。대학에 다닐 땐, 유럽 여행을 상상했지.

When I got there, a woman looked up at me.
我抵達的時候，一位女士抬頭看了我。내가 그곳에 도착했을 때, 한 여자가 나를 올려다봤어.

When I stood, I was struck by a wave of nausea.
當我站著時，我感到一陣噁心。서 있는데, 갑자기 심하게 토할 것 같았어.　＊nausea 噁心，反胃

When I was about your age, my parents got divorced.
當我在你這個年紀的時候，父母離婚了。내가 네 나이 또래일 때, 부모님이 이혼하셨어.

💬 實戰會話

A: **I feel good today.**
我今天心情很好。오늘 기분 좋네.

B: **Do you? You must have done something good.**
你嗎？你肯定做了什麼好事。그래? 뭔가 좋은 일을 했나봐.

A: **How do you know?**
你怎麼知道？어떻게 알아?

B: (　　　　　　　　　　　　　　　　)
做好事讓我心情好。좋은 일을 하면, 기분이 좋지.

A: **I agree with you.**
我同意。같은 생각이야.

Day 8

瘋狂就是
不斷重複同樣的事情

Insanity: doing the same thing over and over again.

today's message

You study hard, but your grades stay the same.
你努力讀書,但成績仍然一樣。열심히 공부해도 성적이 오르지 않나요?

You work hard, but your performance doesn't show any progress.
你努力工作,但工作表現卻沒有任何進展。열심히 일해도 보여줄 만한 성과가 없나요?

Why don't you change the way you study or work?
何不試著改變讀書或工作的方法?공부나 일하는 방법을 바꿔보세요.

You treat people with favor, but it doesn't win any response.
你善待別人,但卻沒有得到任何回應嗎?타인에게 호의를 베풀어도 반응이 없나요?

Why don't you change the way you deal with people?
何不改變你應對別人的方式?사람을 대하는 방법을 바꿔보세요.

It is insane to do the same thing over and over again and expect different results.
不斷的做同一件事卻期待結果有所不同,那是瘋狂。같은 행동을 반복하면서 다른 결과를 기대하는 건 미친 짓이에요.

---

insanity 精神異常 | expect 期待,預期 | stay the same 維持同樣的狀態 | performance 表現,成績,表演,演出 | progress 進展,進度 | treat 應對,對待(人們)| favor 善意 | response 反應,應答 | deal with 對待,處理

正能量英語

Insanity:
doing the same thing
over and over again

Insanity: doing the same thing over and over again

句型 08 Over and over 重複無數次，反覆

Over and over in my mind, I replayed our dancing.
我在心裡，反覆播放著我們舞蹈的畫面。머릿속에서 반복해서, 나는 우리의 춤을 되뇌었어.

Over and over again, I woke up screaming.
我一次又一次的尖叫著醒來。여러 번, 나는 비명을 지르며 잠에서 깼어.

She said it over and over until he calmed again.
她一直重複這句話，直到他冷靜下來。그녀는 그가 다시 진정될 때까지 그 말을 반복했어.

She heard him say it over and over again.
她聽到他不斷重複的說。그녀는 그가 그 말을 계속 반복하는 소리를 들었어.

He apologized over and over.
他不斷的道歉。그는 계속 사과했어.

💬 實戰會話

A: I study hard, but my grades stay the same.
我努力讀書，但成績仍然一樣。열심히 공부했는데, 성적이 그대로야.

B: Then, why don't you change the way you study?
那麼，何不試著改變讀書的方法？그러면, 공부하는 방법을 바꿔보지 그래?

A: Do you think it will work?
你覺得那行得通嗎？효과가 있을까?

B: I'm not sure, but it's worth trying. I think (   ) and expect different results.
我不確定，但是值得嘗試。我覺得不斷的做同一件事卻期待結果有所不同，那是瘋狂。확신은 못하지만, 시도해볼 만한 가치는 있지. 같은 행동을 반복하면서 다른 결과를 기대하는 건 미친 짓이잖아.

Day 9

成功只有一種，
就是你能夠用
自己的方式過一生

There is only one success —
to be able to spend your life in your own way.

today's message

You must want to make a success.
你肯定想成功。성공하고 싶죠.

That's one of everybody's wishes.
那是每個人心中的期許。누구나 성공하고 싶어 하지요.

However, it's hard to define success.
然而,定義成功是困難的。그러나, 무엇이 성공인지 정의하기는 어려워요.

Nevertheless, there's only one success nobody can deny:
不過,有一種沒人可以否定的成功。그럼에도 불구하고, 누구도 부정할 수 없는 유일한 성공이 있어요.

Not to spend your life in other people's ways,
不要將人生耗費在用別人的方式活。당신의 인생을 남의 방식대로 살지 않는 것,

but to be able to spend your life in your own way.
而是用自己的方式過你的人生。당신의 인생을 당신의 뜻대로 살 수 있는 것.

That's success.
那就是成功。그게 바로 성공이에요.

make a success 取得成功 | succeed 成功 | define 定義 | nevertheless 仍然,縱使如此 | deny 否定,否認 | in your own way 照你的方式

正能量英語

There is only one success — to be able to spend your life in your own way.

There is only one success— to be able to spend your life in your own way.

句型 09 There is~ 有~

There is a strange pain in my side.
我側邊有奇怪的疼痛。한 쪽 옆구리에 이상한 통증이 있어.

There is a slight chill in the air.
空氣有點涼涼的。공기가 좀 차네.

There is much to remember.
要記住的有點多。기억할 게 많아요.

There is no explanation for this.
那沒什麼好解釋的。이것에 대한 설명은 없어.

There is nothing I can do.
我沒什麼可以做的。내가 할 수 있는 게 아무것도 없어.

💬 實戰會話

A: It's hard to define success.
定義成功是困難的。성공을 정의하기는 어려워.

B: I know, but I think (　　　　　　　　　　　)
我知道。但我覺得只有一種成功。그렇지. 하지만 난 성공은 딱 하나라고 생각해.

A: What is it?
那是什麼？그게 뭔데?

B: To be able to spend your life in your own way.
就是能夠按照自己的方式生活。네 인생을 네 방식대로 살아갈 수 있는 것.

A: I agree with you.
我同意。맞는 말이야.

Day 10

放下吧！

Just let it go.

today's message

I hear you sigh, 'Life is hard.'
我聽到你感嘆「人生很難」。당신은 한숨 쉬며 살기 힘들다고 해요.

You want to give up.
你想要放棄。포기하고 싶다고요.

Hold on.
撐住。잠깐만요.

What makes you say that?
你怎麼會這樣說？이유를 모르겠군요.

Compared to what?
是跟什麼比較呢？무엇과 비교해서 힘들다는 건가요?

Almost everything is hard in life.
人生中的每件事都是困難的。살다보면 거의 모든 일이 힘들어요.

Just let it go.
就放手吧！그냥 흘러가는 대로 두세요.

You can find yourself in an easier life.
你會發現自己的生活變輕鬆了。더 편안하다고 느낄 거예요.

---

sigh 嘆息 | hard 困難的 | give up 放棄（某件事情） | hold on 暫時等一下 | compare to 與～比較 | let something go 放開（事情）～

正能量英語

Almost everything is
hard in life.
Just let it go.

Almost everything is hard in life. Just let it go.

句型 10　I heard somebody+v. 我聽到～做～

I heard him sigh.
我聽到他嘆息。나는 그가 한숨 쉬는 소리를 들었어.

I heard him complain.
我聽到他抱怨。나는 그가 불평하는 소리를 들었어.

I heard her cry.
我聽到她哭泣。나는 그녀가 우는 소리를 들었어.

I heard her play the piano.
我聽到她彈鋼琴。나는 그녀가 피아노 연주하는 소리를 들었어.

I heard them fight last night.
昨晚我聽到他們吵架。나는 지난 밤에 그들이 싸우는 소리를 들었어.

💬 實戰會話

A: Life is hard.
　　人生好難。살기 힘들어.

B: Life is hard? Compared to what?
　　人生好難？跟什麼比較？살기 힘들다고? 무엇과 비교해서 힘들다는 거야?

A: Well…
　　這個嘛…그게...

B: Almost everything is hard in life.(　　　　　　)
　　You can find yourself in an easier life.
　　人生中的每件事都是困難的。就放手吧！你會發現自己的生活變輕鬆了。
　　살다 보면 거의 모든 게 힘들지. 그냥 흘러가는 대로 둬. 더 편안하다고 느낄 거야.

Positive Quotations
40 days

3week

愛讓我們再次相信

Day 11

療癒
來自於承擔責任

Healing comes from taking responsibility.

today's message

You look like you feel hurt.
你感覺受傷了。마음이 상한 것 같네요.

Don't feel sad.
不要覺得難過。우울해하지 말아요.

Don't feel small.
不要覺得渺小。위축되지 말아요.

Don't whine about anything.
不要對任何事情發牢騷。무엇에 대해서도 하소연하지 말아요.

Healing doesn't come from those ways.
這些方式不會帶來療癒。치유는 그런 식으로 되지 않아요.

Take responsibility for the wounds inside.
為內心的傷口負起責任。마음속 상처들에 책임을 지세요.

Healing comes from taking responsibility.
療癒來自於承擔責任。치유는 책임질 때 되어요.

---

healing 療癒 | take responsibility 負責任 | feel hurt 感覺受傷 | feel small 覺得渺小 | whine 嘀咕著牢騷，哀訴 | wound 傷口 | inside 內部，內心的

正能量英語

Healing comes from taking responsibility.

Healing comes from taking responsibility.

句型 11

come from 來自～，源自於～

The music is coming from the room.
音樂從房間傳出來。음악이 그 방에서 흘러나오고 있어.

Where did the money come from?
這筆錢是從哪裡來的？그 돈은 어디에서 생긴 거야?

I saw flames coming from the engine.
我看到火焰從引擎竄出來。나는 엔진에서 불길이 솟는 걸 봤어.

I've come from Paris to take the job.
我從巴黎來接這個工作。나는 그 일을 하러 파리에서 왔어.

That idea came from me.
這個想法是我想出來的。그 아이디어는 내가 낸 거야.

💬 實戰會話

A: **You look like you feel hurt.**
你看起來很受傷。기분이 상해 보이네.

B: **Yes, I do. I heard people badmouthing me behind my back.**
是的，我聽說有人在背後說我壞話。응, 그래. 사람들이 내 뒤에서 내 험담하는 걸 들었어.

A: **Listen to me. Don't feel sad or small about that. Take responsibility for that instead.**
聽我說。不要覺得難過或者覺得被羞辱，相反的，要為此負責。내 말 잘 들어. 그것 때문에 슬퍼하거나 위축되지 마. 대신 사람들이 그러는 것에 대한 책임을 지도록 해.

B: **Take responsibility?**
負責？책임을 지라고?

A: **Yes. (   )**
沒錯。療癒來自於承擔責任。그래. 치유는 책임질 때 되는 거야.

Day 12

善於傾聽的人
不僅受人歡迎,
還能增廣見聞

A good listener is not only popular everywhere,
but after a while he knows something.

today's message

You have no idea why people keep distance from you.
你不知道人們為什麼跟你保持距離。사람들이 왜 당신을 멀리하는지 모르는군요.

Why don't you reflect on yourself?
你何不回顧一下自己？왜 자신을 비춰보지 않나요?

Do you listen to people?
你聽別人說話嗎？당신은 사람들의 말을 경청하나요?

Don't you speak without listening to others?
你是不是只顧著說卻不聽別人說呢？자기 이야기만 하고 다른 사람의 말을 무시하지는 않나요?

A good listener is popular everywhere.
傾聽別人的人走到哪都受歡迎。남의 말을 경청하는 사람은 어디에서나 인기가 있어요.

And after a while he knows something from listening to people.
並且在一段時間之後，他就會從傾聽別人了解一些事情。그리고 사람들의 말을 경청하다보면 오래지 않아 뭔가를 알게 되지요.

---

popular 受歡迎的，大眾的 | keep distance from 從～保持距離 | have no idea 完全不知道 | listen to 傾聽 | reflect on 反省，回顧

正能量英語

A good listener is not only popular everywhere, but after a while he knows something.

A good listener is not only popular everywhere, but after a while he knows something.

句型 12　after a while 不用多久，不久後

After a while most of us gave up.
不久後大部分的人都放棄了。얼마 후에 우리 중 대부분은 포기했어.

After a while the relationship became bumpier.
這份關係在不久後變得更坎坷。오래지 않아 그 관계는 더욱 평탄치 않게 되었어.

After a while I looked up at the clock.
不久後我抬頭看了時鐘。잠시 후에 난 고개 들어 시계를 봤어.　　*bumpy 坎坷，顛簸

After a while the meeting turned out to be productive.
不久後會議變得有生產力。오래지 않아 그 회의는 생산적으로 바뀌었어.

After a while he turned the limo up a steep hill off the main road.
他在不久後脫離主要幹道，將豪華轎車開往陡坡。잠시 후에 그는 도로에서 벗어나 가파른 언덕으로 리무진을 돌렸어.

💬 實戰會話

A: How are you doing? 你好嗎？잘 지내?
B: I feel a little bad. My coworkers keep distance from me.
我覺得有點不舒服。同事們在排擠我。기분이 별로야. 동료들이 나를 밀리해.
A: Well, to be honest with you, you don't listen to people.
好吧，我就坦白說了，你不聽別人說話。저기, 솔직히 말하자면, 넌 남의 말을 경청하지 않아.
B: Don't I? 我沒有嗎？내가?
A: No, you don't.(　　　　　　　　　　　　)
And while listening to people, you know something.
沒有，你不聽。如果你想受歡迎，你應該當個好的傾聽者。在聽別人說話的同時，你會知道一些事情。응, 그래. 인기가 있으려면 남의 말을 경청할 줄 알아야 돼. 그리고 사람들의 말을 경청하다보 면 오래지 않아 뭔가를 알게 돼.

Day 13

為了理解而傾聽

Do listen to understand.

today's message

You're a good listener.
你是一個好的傾聽者。당신은 상대의 말을 잘 듣습니다.

However, you're still ignored by people.
然而,你依舊被人們忽視。그런데도, 여전히 사람들에게 외면당하나요?

Look at it this way.
用這樣的角度想想。이렇게 한번 생각해 봐요.

What is the reason for you to listen to people?
你傾聽別人的理由是什麼?당신이 사람들의 말을 듣는 이유가 뭔가요?

Do you listen to understand or to reply?
你的傾聽是為了理解,還是回應?상대를 이해하기 위해서인가요, 아니면 상대의 말에 대응하기 위해서인가요?

The biggest communication problem is we do not listen to understand.
溝通最大的問題是,我們不是為了理解而傾聽。소통의 가장 큰 문제는 상대를 이해하기 위해 듣지 않는다는 거죠.

We listen to reply.
我們為了回應而傾聽。우리는 상대의 말에 대응하려고 들어요.

reply 回應 | a good listener 好的傾聽者 | ignore 忽視,不理會 | look at 看,檢查 | this way 以這種方式,用這種方法 | communication 溝通

正能量英語

Do listen to understand.

Do listen to understand.

句型 13 listen to 傾聽

Just listen to me for a minute.
請暫時聽我說。그냥 잠깐 내 말 좀 들어봐.

You don't have to listen to him.
你不用聽他說什麼。넌 그 사람 말은 들을 필요도 없어.

Why aren't you listening to me?
你為什麼不聽我的？왜 내 말을 안 듣고 있니?

I'm not in the mood to listen to you.
我現在沒心情聽你說。난 지금 네 말을 들을 기분이 아니야.

The music is worth listening to.
這個音樂值得聽。그 음악은 들을 만한 가치가 있어.

💬 實戰會話

A: Men and women are so different from each other.
男人跟女人真的太不一樣了。남자와 여자는 서로 너무 달라.

B: In what ways? 從哪方面來說？어떤 면에서?

A: Men don't listen to women to understand. They listen to women just to reply.
男人傾聽女人不是為了理解，而僅僅是為了回應。남자는 여자의 말을 이해하려고 듣는 게 아니야. 그저 대응하려고 듣는 거지.

B: Ah, so you think it causes a communication problem?
喔！所以你覺得這造成溝通上的問題嗎？아, 그래서 그것 때문에 소통에 문제가 생긴다고 생각하니?

A: That's right. ( )
沒錯。溝通最大的問題是，不是為了理解而傾聽。맞아. 소통의 가장 큰 문제는 상대를 이해하기 위해 듣는 게 아니라는 거야.

Day 14

信任是會感染的，
不信任也會

Confidence is contagious. So is the lack of confidence.

today's message

Some people have confidence in people around themselves.
有些人身邊有信任他們的人。주변 사람들을 신뢰하는 사람들이 있지요.

Others don't.
有些人則沒有。그렇지 않은 사람들도 있고요.

What about you?
你呢？당신은 어떤가요?

When I have confidence in others, they have confidence in me.
當我信任別人，別人也會信任我。내가 다른 사람들을 신뢰하면, 그들도 나를 믿어주지요.

When I don't have confidence in others, they don't have any confidence in me.
當我不信任別人，別人也不會信任我。내가 다른 사람들을 신뢰하지 않으면, 그들도 나를 전혀 믿지 않아요.

Confidence is contagious.
信任是會傳染的。믿음은 전염돼요.

So is the lack of confidence.
缺乏信任也是如此。믿지 않음도 마찬가지에요.

---

confidence 信任，信心，確信 | contagious 傳染的，有傳染性的 | lack 缺乏，匱乏

正能量英語

Confidence is contagious.
So is the lack of confidence.

Confidence is contagious. So is the lack of confidence.

句型 14　lack of 缺乏

They don't mind the lack of oxygen.
他們不在意氧氣不足。그들은 산소가 부족한 것을 개의치 않아.

I was staggered by his lack of humility.
我對他的不謙虛感到震驚。난 그가 겸손함이 부족한 것에 깜짝 놀랐어.　　* humility 謙遜

My lack of confidence in him goes back to the fall of 2002.
我對他的不信任要回溯到2002年的秋天。내가 그에 대한 믿음이 부족한 건 2002년 가을로 거슬러 올라가지.

Her lack of patience caused the problem.
缺乏耐心給她惹出了麻煩。그녀의 인내심 부족으로 그 문제가 생긴 거야.

I'm tired from lack of sleep.
我因為睡眠不足而感到疲倦。잠을 못 잤더니 피곤해.

💬 實戰會話

A: Do you have a tendency to have confidence in others?
你是一個傾向於信任別人的人嗎？넌 다른 사람들을 믿는 편이니?

B: Have confidence in others? NO!
信任別人嗎？我不是！다른 사람을 믿냐고? 아니!

A: Why not?　為什麼不？왜?

B: How can you trust in others?
你怎麼可能信任別人？다른 사람들을 어떻게 믿어?

A: (　　　　　　　　　) If you don't believe in others, they don't believe in you.
信任是會感染的。當你不信任別人，別人也不會信任你。믿음은 전염돼. 네가 다른 사람들을 믿지 않으면 그들도 너를 믿지 않아.

Day 15

善心永不落空

You never regret being kind.

today's message

Being kind makes people happy.
親切待人讓人感到開心。친절은 사람들을 기분 좋게 하지요.

Being kind gets people a smile.
親切待人讓人微笑。친절은 사람들을 미소 짓게 해요.

Some people exploit kindness though.
然而有些人喜歡剝削這種善良。어떤 사람들은 친절을 악용하기도 하지요.

That's when kindness backfires.
這就是良善事與願違的時候。그럴 때는 친절이 상처가 되어서 돌아오기도 해요.

Some bad people are surely around us.
我們身邊確實有些壞人。우리 주변에는 나쁜 사람들도 분명히 있지요.

If you, nevertheless, don't fail to be kind, you'll end up being rewarded.
而你，縱使如此，一定要對人和善，你終究會得到回報的。만일 당신이, 그럼에도 불구하고, 친절을 잃지 않는다면, 결국 좋은 일이 생길 거예요.

You never regret being kind.
善心永不落空。친절해서 후회하는 일은 절대 없어요.

---

regret 後悔 | exploit（不當的）利用，剝削 | backfire 產生逆向效果，事與願違 | nevertheless 縱使如此 | end up 以～告終，結果 | reward 補償

正能量英語

You never regret being kind.

You never regret being kind.

句型 15 Don't fail to 一定要做

Don't fail to get there in time.
一定要準時抵達那裡。반드시 제시간에 그곳에 도착해야 돼.

Don't fail to bring it back to me tomorrow.
明天別忘了把東西還給我。잊지 말고 그거 내일 나한테 돌려줘.

Don't fail to text him back.
一定要回覆他簡訊。그에게 꼭 답문자 해줘.

Don't fail to send him an email.
一定要寄電子郵件給他。그에게 잊지 말고 이메일 보내.

Don't fail to carry your umbrella.
別忘了帶雨傘。꼭 우산 가지고 다녀.

💬 實戰會話

A: Do I have to be kind to people?
我必須要親切待人嗎?사람들한테 꼭 친절해야 돼?

B: Yes, you should. Being kind makes people happy.
是,你應該要。親切待人讓人感到開心。그럼, 그래야지. 친절은 사람들을 기분 좋게 하니까.

A: Some people exploit kindness.
有些人惡意利用善良。어떤 사람은 친절을 악용하잖아.

B: Ah, I know what you're talking about, but (   )
嗯,我知道你在說什麼,但是善心永不落空。아, 무슨 말하는지 알겠어. 하지만 친절해서 후회하는 일은 절대 없어.

Positive
Quotations
40days

4 week

一切都會過去

Day 16

所有的逆境都有機會

In the middle of every difficulty lies opportunity.

today's message

You're in the middle of difficulties.
你處於困難之中。지금 곤경에 처해 있군요.

There's no exit in sight.
感覺看不到出口。빠져나갈 구멍이 보이지 않네요.

You're putting the blame on others?
你在怪罪別人嗎?남 탓만 하시겠어요?

Opportunity comes in difficulty.
逆境裡都有著機會。힘들 때 기회가 옵니다.

No challenge, no tension and no opportunity are there in an easy life.
安逸的生活裡沒有挑戰,沒有緊張,也沒有機會。편할 때는 도전도, 긴장감도, 기회도 없지요.

Find opportunity in difficulty and challenge aggressively.
在困境裡找到機會,然後積極的接受挑戰吧!힘들수록 기회를 찾고 과감하게 도전하세요.

In the middle of every difficulty lies opportunity.
所有的逆境裡都有著機會。모든 역경 속에는 기회가 있답니다.

difficulty 困難,逆境 | exit 出口 | in sight 看得見 | put the blame on（對出錯的事情）把責任歸咎於別人 | challenge 挑戰 | tension 緊繃,緊張（感）| aggressively 積極的,有攻擊性的

正能量英語

In the middle of every difficulty lies opportunity.

In the middle of every difficulty lies opportunity.

句型 16

in the middle of ~
在～的過程中，在～的途中

I was standing in the middle of the room.
我站在房間的中央。난 그 방 한가운데 서 있었어.

I woke in the middle of the night and couldn't sleep again.
我在半夜醒來然後就睡不著了。한밤중에 일어나서 다시 잠들 수가 없었어.

I was in the middle of something.
我正在忙一些事情。뭘 좀 하고 있던 중이었어.

We're in the middle of an investigation.
我們正在調查。우리는 지금 한창 조사 중이야.

In the middle of the meeting, his face was red with anger.
在會議中，他的臉因為生氣而漲紅。회의 중에, 그의 얼굴이 화가 나서 벌개졌어.

💬 實戰會話

A: There's no exit in sight.
看不見哪裡有出口。빠져나갈 구멍이 보이지 않아.

B: Well… why don't you look at it this way?
這個嘛…你何不這樣看事情？음... 이런 식으로 생각해보면 어떨까?

A: What is that?
怎麼看？어떻게?

B: Opportunity comes in difficulty. (   )
機會來自困境。所有的逆境裡都有著機會。기회는 힘든 순간에 찾아온다고. 모든 역경 속에는 기회가 있어.

Day 17

挫敗只是一時的

Being defeated is often only a temporary condition.

today's message

Being defeated shouldn't make you depressed.
遭受挫敗不該讓你覺得沮喪。실패했다고 우울해하지 말아요.

Being defeated happens.
失敗是會發生的。실패는 늘 있는 일이에요.

Everybody can be defeated.
每個人都會失敗。누구나 실패할 수 있어요.

However, don't let being defeated turn into giving up.
然而，不要讓挫敗轉變成放棄。하지만, 실패했다고 포기하지는 말아요.

When being defeated is often only a temporary condition,
遭受挫敗常是一時的狀態。패배는 대개 일시적인 현상일 뿐이지만,

giving up makes it permanent.
放棄則會變成永恆。포기를 하면 영원해지지요.

When you give up, you'll have a hard time getting back on your feet.
當你放棄，想重新來過時將會困難重重。포기해버리면, 온전히 재기하기 어렵습니다.

---

be defeated 擊敗，挫敗 | shouldn't ~ 不應該~ | make someone depressed ~ 讓~感到沮喪 | turn into 變成~ | give up 放棄 | temporary 一時的，暫時的 | condition 狀態，情況 | permanent 永遠的 | get back 回來 | on your feet （患病或遭受挫折後）完全復原

正能量英語

Being defeated is often only a temporary condition.

Being defeated is often only a temporary condition.

句型 17 make A+adj. 將A做成～的狀態

I want to make his funeral special.
我希望幫他辦一場特別的告別式。그의 장례식을 특별하게 만들고 싶어.

You're making it worse.
你會讓事情變糟。네가 상황을 더 악화시키고 있잖아.

I'm going to make you proud of me.
我會讓你為我感到驕傲。네가 나를 자랑스러워 하도록 만들 거야.

There's nothing that makes me more nervous than that.
沒有比那個更讓我感到緊張的事情。그것보다 나를 더 긴장되게 만드는 일은 없어.

I don't want the situation to make you uncomfortable.
我不想這種狀況讓你感到不舒服。그 상황 때문에 네가 불편해지는 건 원하지 않아.

💬 實戰會話

A: I'd like to give up.
我想放棄。포기하고 싶어.

B: I know what you mean. But don't give up.
我知道你的意思。但不要放棄。무슨 말인지 알아. 하지만 포기하지 마.

A: Why not?
為什麼不？왜?

B: Being defeated is often only a temporary condition.
遭受挫敗常是一時的狀態。패배는 단지 일시적인 현상일 뿐이야.

(   )
放棄則會變成永恆。포기를 하면 영원해지지.

Day 18

只要堅持夠久，我們就能做到任何想做的事

We can do anything we want
as long as we stick to it long enough.

today's message

You are about to give up on something?
你要放棄了嗎？뭔가를 포기하려 하나요?

It has made you feel down?
這讓你感到低落嗎？마음이 힘들고 꺾이죠?

You're blaming yourself for that?
你因為這樣而自責嗎？그것에 대해 자책도 하고요?

No, don't give up.
不，不要放棄。그러지 마세요, 포기하지 말아요.

Just stick to it.
堅持下去。그냥 계속 밀어붙여요.

Everything needs time.
所有的事情都需要時間。모든 일에는 시간이 필요해요.

You can do anything you want as long as you stick to it long enough.
只要你堅持得夠久，你可以做到任何自己想做的事。포기하지 않고 계속 해나가면 원하는 것은 무엇이든 할 수 있어요.

---

long enough 時間充足 | stick to ~ 堅持，持續做～ | be about to 正準備～ | give up on ~ 放棄～（的期盼），對～失望 | feel down 感覺憂鬱，感覺挫折 | blame oneself 自責

正能量英語

We can do anything we want as long as we stick to it long enough.

We can do anything we want as long as we stick to it long enough.

句型 18　as long as 直到~，只要~

I will never forget this as long as I live.
只要還活著我絕不會忘記。내가 살아 있는 동안 이건 절대 잊지 않을 거야.

You can stay here as long as you like.
你想要待多久都可以。네가 좋은 만큼 여기 머물러도 돼.

I'd be happy to do anything as long as you were with me.
直到你跟我在一起，我樂意做任何事情。네가 나와 함께 한다면 무슨 일이든 기쁘게 할 수 있어.

As long as he doesn't ask about my past, I can meet him.
直到他不過問我的過往，我可以見他。그가 내 과거만 묻지 않는다면, 그를 만날 수는 있지.

As long as you're not busy, get me a Diet Pepsi.
只要你不忙，幫我拿一罐百事健怡可樂。바쁘지 않으면, 다이어트 펩시콜라 좀 갖다 줘.

💬 實戰會話

A: I can't keep going on like this. I can't handle this business any longer.
我沒辦法再這樣了。我再也不能處理這事了。이런 식으로 계속 할 수는 없어. 난 이 일을 더 이상 감당할 수가 없어.

B: Listen. That's not long enough to succeed. Don't blame yourself. You need more time.
聽著，時間不夠長，是無法成功的。不要責怪自己。你需要更多時間。들어봐. 성공하기에 충분한 시간은 아니지. 자책하지 마. 너한테는 시간이 더 필요한 거야.

A: Do you think so?
你這樣覺得嗎？그렇게 생각해?

B: Yes. (　　　　　　　　　　　　　　　　　　　)
是。只要堅持夠久，你就能做到任何想做的事情。그럼. 포기하지 않고 계속 해나가면 원하는 건 뭐든지 할 수 있어.

Day 19

每次歷經逆境，
我們都會被精煉如黃金。

We are refined like gold, with every adversity endured.

today's message

You want to live in a different world?
你想在不同的世界生活嗎？다른 세상에서 살고 싶은가요?

You are wondering why you should bother to live this way?
你想知道自己為什麼要這麼費心生活？왜 이렇게 애를 쓰며 살아야 되나 싶은가요?

You seem to be in adversity.
你似乎處於逆境。지금 역경에 처하신 듯하네요.

In fact, nobody can avoid adversity.
事實上，沒人可以躲過逆境。사실, 역경 없이 살 수 있는 사람은 단 한 사람도 없지요.

If it is true, adversity must be there to be endured.
如果這是真的，逆境是為了承受而存在。그렇다면, 역경은 견뎌내기 위해 존재하는 겁니다.

We are refined like gold.
我們會被精煉如黃金。우리는 금처럼 정제되지요.

With every adversity endured.
藉由經歷過的每一次的磨難。매번 역경을 견디면서요.

refined 精煉，提煉 | adversity 逆境 | endure 忍耐，忍受 | bother 費心 | avoid 逃避

正能量英語

We are refined like gold,
with every adversity endured.

We are refined like gold, with every adversity endured.

句型 19　this way　以這種形式,如此

I knew you were going to react this way.
我知道你會這樣反應。난 네가 이런 식으로 반응할지 알고 있었어.

Think of it this way.
請試著這樣想。그걸 이렇게 한번 생각해봐.

Let me put it this way.
讓我這樣說吧！내가 이렇게 한번 설명해볼게.

We've lived this way always.
我們總是這樣生活。우리는 언제나 이런 식으로 살아왔어.

She never behaves this way.
她不曾這樣行動。그녀는 절대 이런 식으로 행동하지 않아.

💬 實戰會話

A: How can we change this world for the better?
我們該如何讓這個世界變得更好？어떻게 하면 이 세상을 더 좋게 바꿀 수 있을까?

B: You're not satisfied with this world?
你不滿意這個世界嗎？이 세상이 마음에 들지 않아?

A: Never.　從不。절대로.

B: You sound like you're in adversity.
你聽起來像是處在逆境。역경에 처한 사람처럼 들리는걸.

A: In a way, yes.
某種程度上,是的。그렇다고 볼 수도 있지.

B: (　　　　　　　　　　　　　　　　　　　　　　　)
每次歷經逆境,我們都會被精煉如黃金。우리는 금처럼 정제되는 거야. 매번 역경을 견뎌 내면서.

Day 20

持之以恆，
你會戰勝任何情況

With patient persistence,
you will conquer any situation.

today's message

Be more patient.
有耐心一點。조금만 더 인내심을 가져봐요.

You're almost there.
你幾乎快到了。고지가 바로 저긴데.

Don't give in to the temptation of submission.
不要屈服於投降的誘惑。포기의 유혹에 굴복하지 말아요.

Submission looks sweet, but it is extremely bitter.
投降看起來甜蜜，但那是極度苦澀的。포기는 달콤해 보이지만, 쓰디쓰지요.

You need persistence.
你需要韌性。끈기가 필요해요.

Keep going with persistence.
堅韌的持續前進。끈기로 밀고 나가요.

With patient persistence, you will conquer any situation.
持之以恆，你會戰勝任何情況。끈기 있게 버티면, 어떤 상황도 이겨낼 수 있어요.

---

patient 耐心，忍耐 | persistence 韌性，固執 | conquer 戰勝，征服 | give in to ~ 投降，讓步 | temptation 誘惑 | submission 降服，屈服 | extremely bitter 極度苦澀，很苦的

正能量英語

With patient persistence, you will conquer any situation.

With patient persistence, you will conquer any situation.

句型 20　more 更加

I like my apartment for more reasons than one.
我喜歡公寓的理由不只一個。내가 내 아파트를 좋아하는 데는 한 가지 이상의 이유가 있어.

I feel more comfortable. 我感覺更舒服了。마음이 좀 편해.

George Bush was probably even more famous than Tony Blair.
喬治‧布希可能比東尼‧布萊爾更有名氣。조지 부시는 아마도 토니 블레어보다 훨씬 더 유명했을 거야.

I could spend more time on my own.
我可以花更多時間獨處。나 혼자만의 시간을 좀 더 보낼 수 있었지.

Telling a story is more difficult than it looks.
說故事比想像中困難。어떤 이야기를 전달한다는 게 보기보다는 더 어려워.

💬 實戰會話

A: You must be under a lot of pressure.
你肯定承受著很大的壓力。스트레스 많이 받겠네.

B: Yes, I am. 是，我是。네, 그렇죠.

A: You're almost there. Don't give up.
你幾乎快到了，不要放棄。목표까지 거의 다 왔어. 포기하지 마.

B: Sometimes I'm tempted to give up, but I know I must not.
有時我想放棄，但我知道我不能。때로 포기하고 싶은 유혹도 받지만, 포기하면 안 된다는 거 알아요.

A: I'm proud of you. Be more patient. (　　　　　)
我為你感到驕傲。有耐心一點。持之以恆，你會戰勝任何情況。네가 자랑스러워. 좀 더 참아봐. 끈기 있게 버티면 어떤 상황도 이겨낼 수 있어.

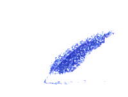

Positive Quotations 40days

5 week

活出自己的價值

Day 21

每個人都應該
立下目標去達成

Everybody should have goals to reach.

today's message

I don't have any goals.
我沒有任何目標。난 목표가 없어요.

What should I do? How should I live?
我該怎麼做？我該怎麼生活？무엇을 해야 하나요? 어떻게 살아가야 하죠?

I don't have those goals.
我沒有那些目標。그런 목표들이 없다고요.

No. That's not the way to live.
不，你不能這樣生活。아니요. 그렇게 살면 안 돼요.

You should have goals.
你應該有目標。목표가 있어야죠.

Everybody should have goals to reach.
每個人都應該立下目標去達成。누구나 이루고자 하는 목표가 있어야 해요.

Life without any goals means nothing.
沒有目標的人生沒有意義。목표가 없으면 삶의 의미도 없어요.

The tragedy of life lies in having no goal to reach.
人生的悲劇就是沒有想完成的目標。삶의 비극은 이룰 목표가 없다는 데 있어요.

---

goal to reach 要完成的目標 | the way to live 生活方式 | mean nothing 沒有意義，不代表任何事情 | tragedy 悲劇 | lie in 在於，存在於

正能量英語

Everybody should have goals to reach.

Everybody should have goals to reach.

句型 21　lie in 在於～

My interest lies in you.
我對你有興趣。나 너한테 관심 있어.

Your future lies in my hands.
你的未來在我手裡。네 미래는 내 손 안에 있어.

His success lies in the results of this case.
他的成功在於這個案子的結果。그의 성공은 이 사건의 결과에 달렸어.

Making success does not lie in making money.
成功不在於賺錢。성공이 돈을 번다는 것을 의미하지는 않아.

Happiness lies in a successful married life.
幸福存在於成功的婚姻生活裡。행복은 성공적인 결혼 생활에 달려 있어.

💬 實戰會話

A: I don't think goals are worth being set.
我不覺得有設定目標的必要。난 목표는 세울 필요가 없다고 생각해.

B: What makes you say that? You think setting goals means nothing?
你怎麼會這樣說？你覺得設定目標沒有任何意義嗎？무슨 소리야? 목표를 세우는 게 아무런 의미가 없다니?

A: Don't misunderstand me. After setting goals, it's hard for you to fulfill them. That's what I mean.
不要誤會。我的意思是說，設定目標之後實踐目標才是困難的。오해하지 마. 목표를 세운 후에 그것들을 이루기가 힘들다는 얘기야. 그 뜻이라고.

B: I know what you mean, but (　　　　) Remember that.
我懂你的意思，但請記住人生的悲劇就是沒有想完成的目標。무슨 말인지 알겠어. 하지만 삶의 비극은 이룰 목표가 없는 데 있어. 기억하라고.

Day 22

如果想要不曾擁有過的東西，就要做不曾做過的事

If you want something you've never had,
then you've got to do something you've never done.

today's message

You want to get a better job?
你想要更好的工作嗎？더 좋은 직장을 원하나요?

You want to get a dream car?
你想擁有夢想中的車子嗎？꿈에 그리던 멋진 차를 갖고 싶나요?

You want to date a nice woman?
你想要跟好女人約會嗎？근사한 여성과 데이트하고 싶나요?

You want to win respect from many people?
你想要贏得許多人的尊敬嗎？많은 사람들의 존경을 받고 싶나요?

You can achieve all of those goals.
你可以成就所有的目標。그 모든 목표를 이룰 수 있어요.

However, if you want something you've never had, you've got to do something you've never done.
然而，如果想要不曾擁有過的東西，就要做不曾做過的事。하지만, 그동안 갖지 못했던 것을 원한다면, 그동안 하지 않았던 것을 해야 하죠.

dream car 夢想中的車 | win respect 贏得尊敬 | achieve 成就，完成

正能量英語

If you want something
you've never had,
then you've got to do
something
you've never done.

If you want something you've never had, then you've got to do something you've never done.

句型 22　You've never+p.p. 你不曾~

It's a city you've never visited.
你不曾造訪過這個城市。거긴 네가 한 번도 가 본 적이 없는 도시야.

You've never realized it.
你不曾理解過這個。그건 그동안 네가 깨닫지 못했던 거야.

You've never said that before.
你過去不曾這樣說。전에 그런 말한 적 없잖아.

You've never heard of him.
你不曾聽說過這個人。넌 그에 대한 이야기를 들어 본 적 없잖아.

You've never experienced it.
你不曾經驗過這個。넌 그런 경험을 해 본 적이 없잖아.

💬 實戰會話

A: I want to get a better job. 我想要一個更好的工作。더 좋은 직업을 갖고 싶어.
B: Oh, you want to change your job?
喔！你想要換工作？오, 직업을 바꾸고 싶어?
A: Yes. And I want to get a dream car.
是，並且我想要夢想中的車子。그래. 그리고 꿈에 그리던 멋진 차를 갖고 싶어.
B: Oh, you need to make a lot of money.
喔！你需要賺很多錢。오, 돈 많이 벌어야겠네.
A: I'd like to date a nice woman.
我想和好女人約會。근사한 여성과 데이트하고 싶어.
B: You know what? (   )
你知道嗎？如果想要不曾擁有過的東西，就要做不曾做過的事。그거 알아? 그동안 갖지 못했던 것을 원한다면 그동안 하지 않았던 것을 해야 해.

Day 23

擁有好點子的最佳方式，就是產生大量的點子

The best way to have a good idea is to have lots of ideas.

today's message

You're not being able to come up with a good idea?
你還沒想出好的點子？좋은 아이디어가 떠오르지 않나요?

A good idea is not coming up as it used to be?
好點子不像以前那麼容易浮現？예전보다 좋은 아이디어도 아니고요?

Are you blaming your age for that?
你因此責怪自己上年紀了嗎？그게 나이 때문이라고 탓하나요?

Do you think a lot as you used to do?
你覺得自己有像以前一樣常常思考嗎？예전만큼 생각을 많이 하나요?

Not being able to have a good idea must mean you don't do a lot of thinking.
沒能想出好的點子，肯定意味著你不像過去那樣頻繁進行思考。좋은 아이디어가 떠오르지 않는 이유는 생각을 많이 하지 않아서일 거예요.

As you can find yourself a right person after you meet many people,
如同見過很多人才能找到適合你的人一樣。나에게 맞는 사람을 찾으려면 많은 사람을 만나봐야 하듯,

you should have lots of ideas to have a good idea.
你必須要擁有很多想法，才能有一個好點子。많은 생각을 하면 좋은 생각이 떠오른답니다.

come up with~ 想出～ | blame ~ 責怪～，向～問責 | do a lot of thinking 做很多的思考

正能量英語

The best way to have a good idea is to have lots of ideas.

The best way to have a good idea is to have lots of ideas.

句型 23　used to（過去）經常～

I used to wear the shirt frequently.
我曾經常穿襯衫。나는 그 셔츠를 자주 입었었어.

I never used to be late.
我不曾遲到。나는 절대 늦은 적이 없었어.

We used to go everywhere together.
我們曾經到哪裡都是一起。우리는 어디든 함께 다녔었어.

I used to be a real loudmouth.
我曾經是愛說大話的人。내가 한때는 완전 떠버리였지.　　　* loudmouth 吹牛，自誇

I'm stronger than I used to be.
我比過去更強壯了。나는 예전보다 힘이 세졌어.

💬 實戰會話

A. I'm short of ideas.
點子不太夠。아이디어가 부족해.

B. But you were full of ideas, weren't you?
但你以前點子很多，不是嗎？그렇지만 너 아이디어 창고였잖아.

A. Used to be, but not these days.
曾經是，但最近不是了。예전에는 그랬는데, 요즘은 아니야.

B. You mustn't think a lot as you used to do.
你肯定不像以前那樣常常思考。예전만큼 생각을 많이 하지 않나봐.

A. I think so.　好像是這樣。그런 것 같아.

B. When (　　　　　　　), you can have a good idea.
當你有很多想法時，你會想出好點子的。생각을 많이 하면, 좋은 아이디어가 생각날 거야.

Day 24

想要活出創意人生，
就不要害怕犯錯

To live a creative life,
you must lose your fear of being wrong.

today's message

You must have thought about living a creative life.
你一定想過活出一個有創意的人生。창의적인 삶을 살고 싶다는 생각을 해봤을 거에요.

You must have thought about living a different life from others.
你一定想過度過一個跟別人不一樣的人生。남들과는 다른 삶을 살고 싶다는 생각도 해봤겠죠.

To act upon those thoughts, you must be bold.
為了將那些想法付諸實踐，你必須果敢。그 생각을 실천하기 위해서는, 과감해야 해요.

You should not let your fear of being wrong hold you back.
你不應該讓害怕犯錯的恐懼綁住你。실패의 두려움에 발목 잡히지 마세요.

The fear ends up preventing you from being creative.
恐懼最終會阻止你成為有創意的。두려움은 결국 창의적이 되는 걸 막지요.

To live a creative life, you must lose your fear of being wrong.
想要活出有創意的人生，就不要害怕犯錯。창의적인 삶을 살기 위해서는, 실패의 두려움에서 벗어나야 해요.

---

lose fear of ~ 擺脫對～的恐懼 | be wrong 犯錯，失敗 | act upon ~ 依照～行動，按照～ | thought 想法 | bold 大膽，果斷 | hold back 制止，阻止

正能量英語

To live a creative life,
you must lose your fear
of being wrong.

To live a creative life, you must lose your fear of being wrong.

句型 24   You must have +p.p. 你肯定做過～

You must have imagined it.
你肯定想像過這個。넌 그걸 상상했던 게 틀림없어.

You must have thought I was such an idiot.
你肯定覺得我是笨蛋。넌 나를 그런 멍청한 놈이라고 생각했던 게 틀림없어.

You must have mistaken me for someone else.
你肯定把我誤認為別人。틀림없이 저를 다른 사람으로 착각하셨네요.

You must have had a terrible time.
你肯定度過一段糟糕的時間。정말 얼마나 힘들었니.

You must have seen him.
你肯定見過他。넌 예전에 그 사람을 만난 게 틀림없어.

💬 實戰會話

A. I want to live a creative life.
我想過有創意的人生。난 창의적인 삶을 살고 싶어.

B. You know what? You must be bold in order to live creatively.
你知道嗎？想過有創意的人生就要變得大膽一點。그거 알아? 창의적인 삶을 살기 위해서는 과감해야 돼.

A. I'm listening.
我在聽。계속해봐.

B. To live a creative life, (   )
想要活出創意人生，就不要害怕犯錯。창의적인 삶을 살기 위해서는, 실패의 두려움에서 벗어나야 한다고.

Day 25

你今日的夢想
將會創造你的未來

Your dreams of today will create your future.

today's message

You don't have dreams?
你有夢想嗎？꿈이 없다고요?

Are you sure you don't have any dreams?
你確定你沒有任何夢想嗎？정말 꿈이 하나도 없나요?

Then you don't have a future.
那麼你沒有未來。그렇다면 미래도 없어요.

Your dreams of today will create your future.
今天的夢想將會創造未來的你。미래는 현재의 꿈이 있기에 가능하지요.

Have dreams.
擁抱夢想吧！꿈을 가지세요.

They don't have to be big.
不需要是什麼大事。거창하지 않아도 괜찮아요.

Even small dreams create your own future.
縱使是小的夢想也能創造屬於你的未來。작은 꿈이라도 당신만의 미래를 만들지요.

Your dreams of today will create your future.
你今日的夢想將會形塑你的未來。오늘의 꿈이 당신의 미래를 만들어요.

create 創造，製造 | future 未來，將來

正能量英語

Your dreams of today
will create your future.

Your dreams of today will create your future.

句型 25 Are you sure~? 你確定要~？

Are you sure you want to do this?
你確定想這麼做嗎？너 이걸 하고 싶은 게 분명해?

Are you sure you don't want tea or coffee?
你確定不要喝茶或咖啡嗎？차도 커피도 마시지 않겠다고?

Are you sure you have nothing to do with this?
你確定你跟這件事情無關嗎？네가 이 일과 아무런 관련이 없는 게 분명해?

Are you sure we should be doing this?
你確定我們應該這麼做嗎？우리가 정말 이 일을 해야 돼?

Are you sure we're going the right way?
你確定我們走對了嗎？우리 지금 제대로 가고 있는 거 확실해?

💬 實戰會話

A: What is your dream?
你的夢想是什麼？네 꿈은 뭐야?

B: Dream? I have no dream.
夢想？我沒有夢想。꿈? 난 꿈이 없어.

A: What? ( )
什麼？你確定沒有夢想嗎？뭐? 꿈이 정말 없어?

B: So what?
那又怎樣？그게 뭐?

A: So what? Your dreams of today will create your future.
會怎樣？你今日的夢想將會創造你的未來。그게 뭐 어떠냐? 오늘의 꿈이 네 미래를 만든다고.

Positive Quotations 40days

6 week

現在,就幸福

Day 26

所有的時間都是相連的，
過去、現在及未來

All times are connected; past, present and future.

today's message

Aren't you wasting your time?
你在浪費時間嗎？시간을 낭비하고 있진 않나요?

Time is so precious.
時間是那麼的珍貴。시간은 정말 소중해요.

Present turns into past in no time.
現在瞬間變成過往。현재가 지나면 바로 과거가 되지요.

Future is just ahead of you.
未來就在你眼前。바로 눈앞에 미래가 있어요.

In other words past, present and future are closely connected.
換句話說，過去、現在以及未來都是緊密相連的。결국 과거와 현재, 미래는 가깝게 이어져 있지요.

You may understand how precious the present is!
你或許知道了現在是何等珍貴！현재가 얼마나 소중한지를 알 수 있을 거에요!

Don't waste your present.
不要浪費現在。현재를 헛되이 보내지 마세요.

---

connected 連接，相關 | precious 貴重的，珍貴的 | turn into （因為轉變）成為～ | in no time 很快，立即 | in other words 換句話說 | closely 緊密地，仔細地

正能量英語

All times are connected; past, present and future.

All times are connected; past, present and future.

句型 26

ahead of
（空間或者時間上的）在～之前

We put business ahead of everything.
我們把事業放在第一順位。우리는 무엇보다도 일을 가장 우선시 해.

He's a year ahead of me.
他比我大一歲。그는 나보다 1년 위야.

He is smart with a good future ahead of him.
他很聰明並且有美好的未來在等著他。그는 똑똑한 데다 그의 앞에는 멋진 미래가 펼쳐져 있어.

From somewhere ahead of us a whistle screeched.
刺耳的哨子聲來自我們的前方。우리 앞에 어디에선가 호각 소리가 들렸어.

We face huge tasks ahead of us.
我們面臨著艱鉅的任務。우리는 엄청난 일들을 직면하고 있어.

* screech 尖叫，刺耳聲

💬 實戰會話

A: You're wasting your time.
你在浪費時間。넌 시간 낭비하고 있어.

B: No, I'm NOT. Playing computer games is not a waste of time.
不，我沒有。玩電腦遊戲不是浪費時間。아니야. 컴퓨터 게임은 시간 낭비가 아니라고.

A: Then what is it? 那是什麼？그러면 뭐야?

B: It's my favorite pastime.
這是我喜歡的娛樂。내가 좋아하는 취미지.

A: Listen to me. Don't waste your present.
你聽我說，不要浪費現在的時間。내 말 들어봐. 현재를 헛되이 보내지 마.

(   )
過去、現在以及未來都是緊密相連的。과거와 현재, 미래는 가깝게 이어져 있다고.

Day 27

如果想要幸福，
請放下過去

If you want to be happy, give up the past.

today's message

How are things going?
事情都還好嗎?요즘 어떻게 지내요?

Sometimes you may think, "Those were the days."
有時你可能會想,「曾經的美好時光啊」。예전만 못하다고 생각할 때가 있죠?

However, don't just reminisce about the past.
然而,不要只追憶那些過往。그렇다고 과거만 회상하며 살진 말아요.

Sometimes the memories can prevent you from moving on.
有時回憶會阻礙你前進。때로는 과거가 당신의 삶을 지지부진하게 만들 수도 있어요.

Don't entangle yourself in the past.
不要被過往綁住。과거에 얽매이지 마세요.

If you want to be happy, give up the past.
如果想要幸福,請放下過去。행복하고 싶다면, 과거를 잊으세요.

give up 放棄 | reminisce 追憶,回憶 | past 過去,過往的事 | move on 前進

正能量英語

If you want to be happy,
give up the past.

If you want to be happy, give up the past.

句型 27　prevent A from B　阻止A做B

Nothing would prevent me from doing that.
沒有任何事可以阻止我做那件事。그 무엇도 내가 그 일을 하는 것을 막지 못할 거야.

I couldn't prevent them from coming.
我無法阻止他們來。나는 그들이 오는 것을 막을 수가 없었어.

His knee injury prevented him from becoming a professional athlete.
他因為膝蓋受傷沒能成為職業運動員。그는 무릎 부상 때문에 전문 육상선수가 되지 못했어.

We have to prevent this from happening.
我們必須阻止這件事情發生。우리가 이 일이 일어나지 않게 막아야 돼.

Prevent her from connecting with anyone.
阻止她聯繫任何人。그녀가 누구와도 연락 못하게 해.

💬 實戰會話

A: Those were the days.
曾經的美好時光啊！옛날이 참 좋았는데.

B: You're at it again.
你怎麼又開始了。또 그런다.

A: I'd like to go back to the past.
我想回到過去的日子。과거로 돌아가고 싶어.

B: Listen. (　　　　　　　　　　　　　　)
聽著。如果想要幸福，請放下過去。잘 들어. 행복하고 싶다면 과거를 잊으라고.

Day 28

原諒不能改變過去，
但是可以擴展未來

Forgiveness does not change the past,
but it does enlarge the future.

today's message

You still don't forgive him.
你依舊不能原諒他。여전히 그를 용서하지 못하네요.

Forgiveness doesn't make any difference?
原諒不能改變任何事嗎？용서해서 달라지는 건 아무것도 없다고요?

No, forgiveness does not change the past.
沒錯，原諒無法改變過去。그래요, 용서가 과거를 바꾸진 않죠.

However, forgiveness enlarges the future.
然而，原諒可以擴展未來。하지만, 용서는 미래를 확장시켜요.

The moment forgiveness swings your closed mind open, your door to the future is wide open.
當原諒打開你緊閉的心，你未來的門也將被敞開。용서가 당신의 닫힌 마음을 열어 젖히는 순간, 미래의 문이 활짝 열리지요.

Forgiveness does not change the past, but it does enlarge the future.
原諒並不能改變過去，但是可以擴展未來。용서가 과거를 바꾸지는 못하지만, 미래는 확장시킨답니다.

---

enlarge 擴充，放大 | make difference 帶來改變，有所作為 | swing open 打開（門快速被打開時使用）| wide open 完全開放的

正能量英語

Forgiveness does not change the past, but it does enlarge the future.

Forgiveness does not change the past, but it does enlarge the future.

句型 28 difference 差距，影響

She won't be able to tell the difference.
她無法分辨出差異。그녀는 차이를 구별할 수 없을 거야.

It makes no difference.
這不會帶來任何改變。그래 봐야 달라지는 건 하나도 없어.

The difference in price is six dollars.
價差是六美元。가격 차이는 6달러야.

The difference was almost impossible to detect.
幾乎無法察覺差異。그 차이를 알아내는 건 거의 불가능해.

* detect 偵測，發現

It is hard to get over the time difference.
真的很難克服時差。시차 극복은 정말 힘들어.

💬 實戰會話

A: I don't think I can forgive him.
我不覺得我可以原諒他。그를 용서하지 못하겠어.

B: But the accident happened last year.
但那是去年的事故。하지만 그 사고는 작년에 있었던 거잖아.

A: I still can't forgive him.
我依舊不能原諒他。그래도 여전히 용서할 수 없어.

B: I think you'd better forgive him and get out of the past.
我覺得你最好可以原諒他然後放下過去。네가 그를 용서하고 과거에서 벗어났으면 좋겠어.

A: Forgiveness doesn't change the past.
原諒並不能改變過去。용서가 과거를 바꾸진 않잖아.

B: I know, (   )
我知道，但是可以擴展未來。알아, 하지만 용서는 미래를 확장시키지.

Day 29

生命不在於長度，
而在於深度

Life is not measured by its length, but by its depth.

today's message

Have you thought about living longer?
你曾想過活久一點嗎?오래 사는 것을 생각하셨나요?

However, just living longer may not make you happier.
然而,僅僅延長生命並不能讓你過得更快樂。하지만, 그저 더 오래 산다고 더 행복한 건 아니에요.

The length of life doesn't measure your life.
生命的長短不能衡量你的人生。삶의 길이가 당신의 삶을 평가하지는 않지요.

A meaningful and profound life you live is more important.
更重要的是活出有意義並深刻的人生。의미 있고 깊이 있는 삶을 사는 것이 더 중요해요.

The depth of life can't be found in a selfish life.
自私的生命裡,看不見生命的深度。인생의 깊이는 이기적인 삶에서는 찾을 수 없어요.

With depth, not length, live your meaningful life.
以深度而非長度,活出有意義的人生。길이가 아닌 깊이로, 의미 있는 삶을 살아보세요.

measure 測量,衡量 | length 長度 | depth 深度 | meaningful 有意義的 | profound 深刻的,淵博的 | selfish 自私的

正能量英語

Life is not measured by
its length,
but by its depth.

Life is not measured by its length, but by its depth.

句型 29 Have you~? 你有~?

Have you heard from him lately?
你最近跟他聯絡嗎?너 요즘 그에게 소식 들었어?

Have you talked to anyone about that?
你有跟任何人討論過這個嗎?너 그것에 대해 누구와 이야기한 적 있어?

Have you noticed how small it is?
你有注意到這個有多小嗎?너 그게 얼마나 작은지 봤어?

Have you ever seen that picture?
你有看過那張照片嗎?너 그 사진 본 적 있어?

Have you seen all your family?
你見到全家人了嗎?너 가족들은 모두 만나봤어?

💬 實戰會話

A: Life expectancy is increasing. Do you want to live longer?
人的預期壽命持續在增長。你想活久一點嗎?평균수명이 점점 늘어나고 있어. 넌 더 오래 살고 싶어?

B: Yes, but just living longer doesn't make people happier, I think.
想。但我認為僅是活得久,不會讓人變得更快樂。응. 하지만 단지 오래 산다고 더 행복한 건 아니라고 생각해.

A: You can say that again. 我完全同意。맞는 말이야.

B: The length of life doesn't measure your life.
生命的長短,並非衡量人生的標準。삶의 길이가 네 삶을 평가하지는 않.

A: Couldn't agree with you more.
(   )
再同意不過了。生命不在於長度,而在於深度。정말 옳은 말이야. 인생은 길이가 아니라 깊이로 평가돼.

Day 30

知足常樂

Be happy with what you have.

today's message

It's hard to be satisfied.
知足很難。만족하기 참 힘들죠.

You keep wanting something else.
你總是想要更多。계속 뭔가를 더 원하게 됩니다.

Sometimes it can be annoying.
有時這會讓人感到厭煩。때때로 짜증나기도 하지요.

Why don't you try to feel happy with what you have?
何不試著對你擁有的感到開心？왜 가진 것에 만족하려 하지 않나요?

When you're happy with what you have, what you want is an extra bonus to you.
當你對擁有的東西感到快樂，你想要的就是額外的獎勵。가진 것에 만족하고, 원하는 것까지 있다면 그건 덤이에요.

Be happy with what you have. Be excited about what you want.
知足常樂。對你想要的感到期待。가진 것에 만족하세요. 원하는 것이 있음에 설레어 하세요.

---

be satisfied 滿足 | something else 別的東西 | annoying 討厭的，惱人的 | Why don't you ~?（提議）你何不～？ | be excited about ~ 對～興奮

正能量英語

Be happy with what you have.

Be happy with what you have.

句型 30 happy with
對～感到滿意，對～感到開心

You don't seem happy with me lately.
你最近好像對我不太滿意。넌 요즘 나한테 만족하지 못하는 것 같아.

I'm happy with the way things are going.
我對事情的發展感到滿意。난 요즘 돌아가는 상황에 만족해.

I'm wondering if she's happy with her husband.
我不確定她跟先生過得好不好。그녀가 남편과 잘 지내는지 모르겠어.

I'm happy with the results.
我對結果感到滿意。난 그 결과에 만족해.

I'm not happy with his frequent trips.
他經常出差，令我不太開心。난 그의 잦은 여행이 싫어.

💬 實戰會話

A: Are you happy with what you have?
你對自己擁有的東西感到滿意嗎？네가 가진 것에 만족하니?

B: What I have? I don't think I have enough.
我擁有的？我想我有的不多。내가 가진 것? 난 충분히 가지지 못했어.

A: You sound like you need something else all the time.
聽起來你總是不滿足。말하는 걸 들으니 넌 늘 뭔가 새로운 게 필요한가 보구나.

B: I think so. Am I wrong?
好像是。我錯了嗎？그런 것 같아. 내가 잘못된 걸까?

A: No, I didn't say that, but you need to (   )
不是，我沒這樣說，但是你需要對擁有的感到滿足。아니, 그런 의미로 말한 건 아니야. 하지만 네가 가진 것에 만족할 필요는 있어.

Positive
Quotations
40days

7week

肯定自己

Day 31

你出生的那一天，
就被賦予了創造自己的力量

The day you were born
you were given power to create yourself.

today's message

You feel lethargic these days?
你最近覺得毫無生氣嗎？요즘 왠지 무기력한가요?

You don't feel any interest in your life.
人生中沒有任何事情令你感到興趣。사는 게 재미없나요?

Aren't you condemning yourself to mediocrity?
你自甘平庸嗎？현실에 안주하는 것 아닐까요?

You have power to create yourself.
你有創造自己的力量。당신에겐 스스로를 창조할 수 있는 힘이 있어요.

You mustn't be using that power.
你一定沒有使用那個力量。그 힘을 전혀 쓰질 않는군요.

When you create yourself, your life regains its energy.
當你創造自己，你的人生會重新獲得能量。스스로를 창조할 때, 삶에 활력이 생겨요.

The day you were born you were given power to create yourself.
你出生的那一天，就被賦予了創造自己的力量。당신이 태어난 날, 당신은 스스로를 창조할 수 있는 힘을 받았어요.

---

create oneself 創造自己，成為新的人 | lethargic 無生氣的，無精打采的 | condemn to 宣告，宣判 | mediocrity 平凡，平庸 | regain 重新獲得，找回

正能量英語

The day you were born
you were given power to
create yourself.

The day you were born you were given power to create yourself.

句型 31　I feel~ 我有~的感覺

I feel guilty already for having awoken you.
不好意思把你吵醒了。너를 깨운 것 때문에 이미 죄책감이 들어.

I feel bad about something.
我對某件事感到難過。뭔가 기분이 나빠.

Showered and dressed, I feel ready to begin this adventure.
沐浴更衣完，我準備開始這場探險了。샤워를 하고 옷을 입으니, 이 모험을 시작할 준비가 된 것 같아.

I feel almost giddy with happiness.
因為開心我幾乎感覺暈眩。행복감에 아찔할 정도야.
＊giddy暈眩的，使人眼花的

I feel compelled to look back on my life.
我不得不回顧自己的一生。억지로라도 내 삶을 되돌아봐야 한다는 기분이 들어.
＊compel受迫的，非自願的

💬 實戰會話

A: I don't feel any interest in my life.
人生讓我覺得無趣。사는 게 재미가 없어.

B: Aren't you condemning yourself to mediocrity?
你在自甘平庸嗎？현실에 안주하는 거 아니야?

A: You mean I seem satisfied with the present?
你是說我好像對現狀感到滿足嗎？내가 현재에 만족하는 것 같다고?

B: That's right. You need to (　　　　　　　　　　)
沒錯。你需要創造自己。그래. 스스로를 창조할 필요가 있어.

Day 32

通往成功的重要關鍵是自信；
而自信的重要關鍵在於準備

One important key to success is self-confidence.
An important key to self-confidence is preparation.

today's message

One important key to success is self-confidence.
通往成功之路的重要關鍵是自信。 성공의 중요한 한 가지 열쇠는 자기 확신이에요.

Self-confidence is confidence that you can do something well.
自信意味著你有信心把某件事情做好。 자기 확신은 뭔가를 잘할 수 있다는 확신이죠.

However, self-confidence doesn't grow by itself.
然而，自信不會自己形成。 하지만, 자기 확신은 저절로 생기지 않아요.

Self-confidence develops when you're prepared.
當你準備好時，自信就會增長。 자기 확신은 준비가 되었을 때 생겨요.

Self-confidence without preparation is arrogance.
未經充分準備而有的自信，就是傲慢。 준비되지 않은 자기 확신은 오만이에요.

An important key to self-confidence is preparation.
自信的重要關鍵在於準備。 자기 확신의 중요한 열쇠는 준비입니다.

confidence 信任，自信 | develop 生長，發達 | by itself 自動地，單獨地 | arrogance 傲慢 | be prepared 準備好的 | preparation 準備

正能量英語

One important key to success is self-confidence. An important key to self-confidence is preparation.

One important key to success is self-confidence. An important key to self-confidence is preparation.

句型 32   key to ～的關鍵

What's the key to success?
什麼是成功的關鍵？성공의 열쇠는 뭘까?

It will be a key to creating innovative economies in the twenty-first century.
這將會成為開創21世紀創新經濟的關鍵。그것은 21세기 혁신 경제를 창조할 열쇠가 될 거야.

It is a key to the higher education market.
這將是高等教育市場的關鍵。그것이 고등교육 시장의 열쇠야.

The key to future success is to not be discouraged about your past or present.
通往未來成功的關鍵是，不要因為過去與現在感到卻步。미래 성공의 열쇠는 과거나 현재에 낙담하지 않는 거야.

Forgiveness is the key to being free from resentment.
從憎恨獲得自由的關鍵是原諒。용서는 분노로부터 자유로워지는 열쇠야.

* resentment 憎恨，怨恨

💬 實戰會話

A: What should I do to develop self-confidence?
我該做什麼才能培養自信？어떻게 해야 자신감이 생기지?

B: Make yourself well-prepared.
讓自己變成一個準備好的人。네 스스로 잘 준비해야지.

A: You mean when I'm well-prepared, my self-confidence develops?
你是說當我準備好，就可以培養自信？잘 준비된 상태일 때, 자신감이 생긴다는 거야?

B: That's right. (   )
沒錯。自信的重要關鍵在於準備。맞아. 자신감의 중요한 열쇠는 준비야.

Day 33

當你說你做得到,
你就釋出了內在創造力

When you say you can,
you free the creative powers in you.

today's message

No, I can't do that.
不,我不能做。아니, 그건 할 수 없어요.

I'm not up to it. I can't.
我做不到。我不行。그건 내가 할 수 있는 일이 아니에요. 난 못해요.

You're always like that.
你總是這樣。항상 그런 식이지요.

You always say you can't.
你總是說你做不到。늘 할 수 없다고 말하죠.

You know what?
你知道嗎?그거 알아요?

When you say you can't, you stop the creative powers in you.
當你說你做不到,你阻斷了內在的創造力。할 수 없다고 말하는 순간, 당신 안의 창의력은 멈춰요.

When you say you can, you free the creative powers in you.
當你說你做得到,你就釋出了內在創造力。할 수 있다고 말하는 순간, 당신 안의 창의력은 자유로워지죠.

---

free 使自由 | creative power 創造力 | be up to ~ 能做到~ | like that 以那種形式 | stop 停止,阻止

正能量英語

When you say you can,
you free
the creative powers
in you.

When you say you can, you free the creative powers in you.

句型 33 I can't~ 我不能做~

I can't afford a car.
我買不起車。난 차 살 돈이 없어.

I can't say any more than that.
我不能說更多了。난 그 이상은 말할 수 없어.

I can't make promises.
我不能做出承諾。난 약속할 수 없어.

I can't tell you where I'll be tomorrow.
我不能告訴你明天我會在哪。난 내일 어디에 있을지 네게 말해줄 수 없어.

I can't be with you tonight.
我今晚不能跟你一起。난 오늘 밤 너와 함께 있을 수 없어.

💬 實戰會話

A: Can you do this for me? I'm sure you can handle it.
你可以幫我嗎？我相信你可以處理好。이거 내 대신 좀 해줄 수 있어? 네가 분명히 처리할 수 있는 일이야.

B: Well… I don't think I can do it. It's beyond my ability.
這個嘛…我不覺得我能做。這超過我的能力。그게… 못하겠는걸. 내 능력으로는 무리야.

A: Come on. You're underestimating your ability.
拜託，你低估自己的能力。왜 그래. 넌 네 능력을 과소평가하고 있어.

B: Do you think so?
你這樣覺得？그렇게 생각해?

A: Yes. (   )
對。當你說你做得到，你就釋出了內在創造力。그래. 할 수 있다고 말하는 순간, 네 안의 창의력이 자유로워진다고.

Day 34

贏得勝利的人，是那些覺得自己做得到的人

Those who win are those who think they can.

today's message

Sometimes you can get depressed.
有時你會變得沮喪。의기소침해질 때가 있지요.

Sometimes you don't think you can make it.
有時你不覺得自己做得到。무언가를 해낼 수 없다고 생각될 때도 있고요.

Sometimes you want to stop everything you've been doing.
有時你想停止手頭在忙的一切。그동안 해오던 모든 걸 멈추고 싶기도 하지요.

Wait, don't stop your goals.
等等，不要停止你的目標。잠깐, 그렇다고 자신의 목표를 멈추지는 말아요.

Think you can make it through thick and thin.
要覺得你在任何情況下都做得到。어떠한 힘든 상황도 이겨낼 수 있다고 생각하세요.

Everybody can't be a winner.
不可能每個人都是贏家。모든 사람이 승자가 될 수는 없어요.

Those who win are those who think they can.
贏得勝利的人，是那些覺得自己做得到的人。할 수 있다고 생각하는 사람이 승리한답니다.

---

get depressed 感到沮喪，感到消沉 | through thick and thin 在任何情況下 | winner 贏家

正能量英語

Those who win are those who think they can.

Those who win are those who think they can.

句型 34 Those who~ 那些~的人

Those who work out stay healthy.
運動的人會維持健康。평소에 운동하는 사람들은 건강을 유지해.

* upper hand 占上風

Those who speak good English have the upper hand.
英文流利的人擁有優勢。영어를 잘하는 사람이 주도권을 잡는 거야.

Those who have worked with him speak highly of him.
跟他工作的人都讚美他。그와 함께 일했던 사람들은 그를 굉장히 칭찬해.

Those who live in Seoul can apply for the job.
住在首爾的人可以應徵這份工作。서울에 사는 사람들이 그 일에 지원할 수 있어.

Those who love music live longer.
熱愛音樂的人長壽。음악을 사랑하는 사람들이 더 오래 살아.

💬 實戰會話

A: I want to stop everything I've been doing.
我想停止手頭在忙的一切。그동안 해오던 일들을 다 그만두고 싶어.

B: Come on. I think you've been doing well.
拜託，我覺得你一直做得很好。무슨 소리야. 그동안 잘해왔잖아.

A: No, no. I don't think I can make it.
不，沒有。我不覺得我做得到。아니, 아니야. 제대로 해내지 못할 것 같아.

B: Don't say that. You can make it through thick and thin.
不要這樣說。你在任何情況下都做得到。그런 소리 마. 넌 아무리 힘들어도 이겨낼 수 있어.

A: But… 但是…하지만…

B: Don't say buts. (   )
別但是了。贏得勝利的人，是那些覺得自己做得到的人。하지만이라고 말하지 마. 할 수 있다고 생각하는 사람이 승리한다고.

Day 35

失敗是可以
重新學習的機會

Failure is an opportunity to learn again.

today's message

You want to work for yourself.
你想創業。독립하고 싶다고요.

That's a good idea.
那是好想法。좋은 생각이에요.

Challenge is there to be taken.
挑戰是為了被接受而存在。도전은 하라고 있는 거니까요.

However, you're afraid of failure.
然而，你害怕失敗。하지만, 실패할까봐 망설이네요.

When the thought of failure keeps you from taking any chance, challenges do not exist.
當對失敗的恐懼阻止你抓住任何機會，挑戰就不會存在。실패가 두려워 도전을 못하면, 도전 자체가 존재할 수 없죠.

Don't be afraid of failure.
不要害怕失敗。실패를 두려워 말아요.

Failure is an opportunity to learn again.
失敗是可以重新學習的機會。실패는 다시 배울 수 있는 기회에요.

---

work for oneself 創業 | take challenge 接受挑戰 | failure 失敗 | keep A from B 阻止 A 做 B | take a chance 碰運氣（冒險）| exist 存在

正能量英語

Failure is an opportunity to learn again.

Failure is an opportunity to learn again.

句型 35 afraid of 擔心~

That's not what I'm afraid of.
我擔心的不是那個。난 그게 두려운 게 아니야.

There's nothing more to be afraid of.
不用再擔心什麼。더 이상 두려울 게 없어.

Of all the things she is afraid of, this is probably number one.
在她擔心的所有事情裡,這可能是她最擔心的。그녀가 두려워하는 모든 것 중에서 이게 아마 최고일 거야.

She's always been afraid of me getting hooked on drugs.
她總是擔心我會對藥物上癮。그녀는 내가 마약에 중독될까 늘 두려워했어.

* hooked on ~ 無法停止,上癮的

I'm afraid of discussing it with him.
我害怕跟他討論這個。난 그 문제를 그와 상의하는 게 두려워.

💬 實戰會話

A: I'm going to work for myself.
我打算創業。직접 회사를 한번 차려보려고.

B: Sounds good.
很棒!좋지.

A: But I'm afraid of failure.
但我害怕失敗。하지만 실패할까 두려워.

B: Don't be afraid of failure. (   )
不要害怕失敗。失敗是可以重新學習的機會。실패를 두려워 마. 실패는 다시 배울 수 있는 기회야.

*Positive
Quotations
40 days*

8week

準備好的幸運

Day 36

成功
是站在失败的肩膀上

Success sits on a mountain of mistakes.

today's message

Mistakes can't be a pride.
犯錯不能成為驕傲。실수가 자랑은 아니죠.

But they don't have to make you depressed either.
但犯錯也不一定會讓你感到沮喪。하지만 그렇게 기죽을 필요도 없어요.

Don't be afraid of making mistakes.
不要害怕犯錯。실수하는 걸 두려워하지 말아요.

Mistakes teach success.
從錯誤中學習，才能成功。실수는 성공을 가르쳐준답니다.

Mistakes get you closer to success.
犯錯是通往成功的必經之路。실수할수록 성공에 점점 가까워지죠.

Don't let yourself get depressed.
不要讓自己感到沮喪。좌절하지 마세요.

Success sits on a mountain of mistakes.
成功是站在失敗的肩膀上。성공은 산더미같이 쌓인 실수 위에 있어요.

pride 自豪，得意 | depressed 沮喪的，消沉的 | get someone closer to ~ 更靠近~

正能量英語

Success sits on a mountain of mistakes.

Success sits on a mountain of mistakes.

句型 36 don't have to 不必~

You don't have to go to that.
你不必去那裡。거기에 꼭 갈 필요는 없어.

You don't have to stay long.
你不必待太久。오래 머물 필요는 없어.

You don't have to do that.
你不一定要做。그럴 필요 없어.

I don't have to go to work.
我不一定要去工作。난 출근할 필요 없어.

We don't have to worry about that part yet.
我們還不用擔心那個部分。우리 아직 그 부분은 걱정할 필요 없어.

💬 實戰會話

A: I made a mistake again. I don't think I can make it.
我又犯錯了。我不覺得我做得到。나 또 실수했어. 난 그거 못할 것 같아.

B: Come on. Mistakes teach success.
拜託,從錯誤中學習,才能成功。왜 이래. 실수가 성공을 가르치는 거야.

A: Excuse me?
你說什麼?뭐라고?

B: Mistakes get you closer to success. (   )
犯錯是通往成功的必經之路。成功是站在失敗的肩膀上。실수들이 성공에 가깝게 해준 다고. 성공은 산더미같이 쌓인 실수 위에 있어.

Day 37

機會總是會來。
打開門迎接機會吧！

Opportunity is always coming.
Open the door and meet opportunity.

today's message

Does opportunity bother to come to me?
機會會來找我嗎?나한테 기회가 올까요?

No, I don't think so.
不,我不這麼認為。아니, 그건 아닐 거예요.

Come on, you should change your mind.
拜託,你該換個想法了!봐요, 생각을 바꿔요.

Opportunity is always coming. To anybody.
機會總是會來,對任何人都是。기회는 항상 와요. 누구에게나요.

But it never knocks on the door.
但機會從不敲門。하지만 기회는 문을 두드리지 않죠.

When you just sit and wait for opportunity to come, you can never get it.
當你坐等機會找上門,你絕對等不到機會。단지 앉아서 기회가 오기만을 기다린다면, 기회를 절대 잡을 수 없어요.

Get yourself prepared and get up.
準備好,然後行動起來!준비하세요. 그리고 일어나세요.

Open the door and meet opportunity.
打開門迎接機會吧!문을 열고 기회를 맞이하세요.

---

get up 站起來 | bother 打擾,擔心 | change one's mind ~ 改變 (某人) 的想法 | get oneself prepared ~ 讓 (某人) 做好準備 | meet 迎接,遇見

正能量英語

Opportunity is
always coming.
Open the door
and meet opportunity.

Opportunity is always coming. Open the door and meet opportunity.

句型 37 You have to~ 你必須要做~

You have to go home just now.
你現在馬上回家。넌 지금 바로 집에 가야 해.

You have to start your life again.
你必須重新開始你的人生。넌 네 인생을 다시 한번 시작해야 해.

You have to tell me why me.
你要告訴我為什麼是我。넌 왜 그게 나인지 말해줘야 돼.

You have to stay with me.
你要跟我在一起。넌 나하고 함께 있어야 돼.

You have to believe in me.
你要相信我。넌 나를 믿어야 돼.

💬 實戰會話

A: Opportunity can come to you.
機會終將到來。네게도 기회는 올 거야.

B: No, I don't think so. It never comes to me.
不,我不這麼覺得。機會不曾來過。아니, 난 그렇게 생각 안 해. 절대 나한테는 안 와.

A: (   ) But it never knocks on the door.
機會永遠都會來,但機會絕不會敲門。기회는 항상 누구에게나 와. 하지만 절대 문을 두드리지는 않지.

B: Then what should I do?
那我該怎麼做?그러면 내가 어떻게 해야 되는데?

A: You should get yourself prepared and get up. Open the door and meet opportunity.
你應該準備好,然後行動起來!打開門迎接機會。준비하고 일어나야 해. 문을 열고 기회를 맞이하라구.

Day 38

名聲是煙霧，人氣是偶然，唯一能持續的只有品性

Fame is vapor, popularity is an accident.
Only one thing endures. And that is character.

today's message

Don't admire fame.
不要羨慕名聲。명성을 흠모하지 말아요.

Fame is vapor.
名聲是煙霧。명성은 증기에요.

Popularity is not planned or intended.
受歡迎不是被計畫好或是被預期的。인기는 계획되거나 의도되지 않죠.

Popularity is an accident.
受歡迎是偶發的。인기는 우연이에요.

Then what endures?
那什麼是持續的？그러면 뭐가 지속적이냐고요?

Only one thing endures.
持續的只有一件事情。지속적인 건 단 하나뿐이랍니다.

And that is character.
只有品格是持續的。그건 품성이에요.

---

fame 名聲 | vapor 水蒸氣，煙霧 | popularity 受歡迎 | accident 偶然，事故 | admire 欽佩，欣賞 | intended 被預期的 | character 個性，品性

正能量英語

Fame is vapor, popularity is an accident. Only one thing endures. And that is character.

Fame is vapor, popularity is an accident. Only one thing endures. And that is character.

句型 38 endure 持續；忍耐

Our love and respect has endured and grown.
我們的愛與尊敬持續並且不斷增長。우리의 사랑과 존경은 지속되었고 더욱 커졌어.

I couldn't endure such pain.
我不能忍受這種疼痛。난 그런 통증은 견딜 수 없었어.

Their friendship endured over many years.
他們的友誼持續了數年。그들의 우정은 여러 해 동안 지속되었어.

I can't endure being apart from you.
我不能忍受跟你分開。난 당신과 떨어져 지내는 건 견딜 수 없어.

There is no way they will endure two weeks of trial.
他們無法熬過兩週的審判。그들은 2주 간의 재판을 견딜 방법이 없어.　　* trail 審問，審判

💬 實戰會話

A: I'd like to win fame and popularity.
我想贏得名聲與人氣。명성과 인기를 얻고 싶어.

B: Nobody would refuse them.
沒人能抗拒這些。그걸 거부하는 사람은 없지.

A: But I don't think you're interested in them.
但我不覺得你對這些感興趣。하지만 넌 그런 것들에 별 관심이 없는 것 같아.

B: No, I'm not.
對，我沒興趣。응. 없어.

A: Why not?
為什麼？왜?

B: (　　　　　　　　　　　　　　　　　　　　　　)
名聲是煙霧，人氣是偶然。명성은 증기야, 인기는 우연이고.

Day 39

不要害怕受傷

Don't be afraid of being hurt.

today's message

Taking chances is intimidating.
冒險是嚇人的。모험을 하는 건 두렵지요.

However, without taking chances you don't understand life.
然而,不冒險你就無法理解人生。하지만, 모험을 하지 않으면 인생을 이해할 수 없어요.

Don't be afraid of being scared.
不要害怕受到驚嚇。겁먹는 걸 두려워하지 마세요.

Don't be afraid of being embarrassed.
不要害怕丟臉。창피함을 두려워하지 마세요.

Don't be afraid of being hurt.
不要害怕受傷。상처 입기를 두려워하지 마세요.

If you've never been scared or embarrassed or hurt,
如果你不曾被嚇到、丟臉或受傷。두렵거나 창피하거나 상처를 입은 경험이 없다면,

it means you've never taken any chances.
這表示你不曾冒過險。당신은 전혀 모험을 하지 않는다는 의미에요.

---

take chances 冒險 | intimidating 嚇人的,脅迫的 | scare 驚嚇,受驚 | embarrass 使局促不安,使尷尬

正能量英語

If you've never been scared or embarrassed or hurt, it means you've never taken any chances.

If you've never been scared or embarrassed or hurt, it means you've never taken any chances.

句型 39　It means~ 這表示~

It means something bad happened to him.
這表示他發生了不好的事情。그건 그에게 뭔가 나쁜 일이 생겼다는 걸 의미해.

It means that I'm moving soon.
這表示我很快要搬家了。내가 곧 이사할 거라는 의미야.

It means that I don't love her.
這表示我不愛她。내가 그녀를 사랑하지 않는다는 의미야.

It means my income will only be eighty dollars a week.
這表示我每週只有八美元的收入。내 수입이 1주일에 단지 80달러밖에 되지 않을 거라는 의미야.

It means I'm sick and tired of him.
這表示我對他感到厭煩。내가 그에게 질렸다는 의미야.

💬 實戰會話

A: Why don't you try it?
你何不試試？그거 한 번 해보지 그래?

B: I'm scared.
我害怕。두려워.

A: Of what?
怕什麼？뭐가?

B: Of failing.
怕失敗。실패할까봐.

A: Come on. (　　　　　　　　　　)
拜託。不要害怕受傷。이것 봐. 상처 입기를 두려워 마.

Day 40

樂在其中
就會帶來成功

Enjoying what we are doing leads to success.

today's message

You must have a hard time in your work.
你的工作肯定很辛苦吧！하고 있는 일이 힘들죠.

You enjoy your work, though.
然而你卻享受工作。그런데도 일을 즐기네요.

When your work gives you a hard time without any happiness, it must be a torture.
當工作只有辛苦沒有快樂，那簡直是折磨。즐거움 없이 일이 힘들기만 하다면, 그건 정말 고통이죠.

We should find work that is enjoyable.
我們應該找可以享受的工作。즐길 수 있는 일을 찾아야 해요.

That's when we think productively and creatively.
那時，我們的思維才會更具生產力與創造力。그래야 생산적이고 창의적인 생각을 하게 되죠.

Being creative leads to success.
具創意會帶來成功。창의적이어야 성공할 수 있어요.

People rarely succeed unless they enjoy what they are doing.
除非享受工作，否則很難取得成功。하고 있는 일을 즐기지 못하면 성공할 가능성은 희박해요.

---

have a hard time 度過辛苦的時間，受苦 | torture 折磨，拷問 | productively 有生產力 | creatively 有創意地 | rarely 很少，難得 | unless 除非

正能量英語

Enjoying what we are doing leads to success.

Enjoying what we are doing leads to success.

句型 40　lead to 通往～

The unfamiliar street leads to another and another.
陌生的街道不斷通往陌生的路。낯선 길을 따라가니 또 다른 낯선 길들로 이어지더군.

The glass doors lead to the terrace.
玻璃門通往庭園。그 유리문들을 따라가면 테라스가 나와.

This will lead to the biggest corporate merger.
這將會帶來最大的企業合併。이건 결국 유례없는 대형 기업합병에 이르게 될 거야.

One call could lead to his bankruptcy.
一通電話可以讓他破產。전화 한 통이면 그는 파산할 수도 있어.

The case could lead to a handsome fee.
這個案子會帶來相當可觀的費用。그 사건을 맡으면 많은 수임료를 받을 수 있어.

* handsome 英俊的，（數量上）相當大的

💬 實戰會話

A: How's your new job?
新工作怎麼樣？새로운 일은 어때?

B: I'm having a hard time, but I like it.
有點累，但我喜歡。힘들긴 한데, 마음에 들어.

A: You sound like (　　　　　　　　　　　　)
你聽起來樂在其中。일을 즐기는 것 같네.

B: Yes, I do. I'm happy with my job.
沒錯。工作讓我感到滿意。응, 맞아. 일이 만족스러워.

A: Happy to hear that. When your work is enjoyable, you can think productively and creatively.
很開心聽到你這樣說。當你樂在工作，你的思考就會變得有生產力與創造力。그 말을 들으니 좋다. 일이 즐거워야, 생산적이고 창의적인 생각을 할 수 있으니까.

*Positive
Quotations
40 days*

實戰會話解答

1 week

- Day 1 It doesn't matter how slow you go as long as you don't stop.
- Day 2 To get out of difficulty, you must go through it.
- Day 3 You can do anything.
- Day 4 Love like you've never been hurt.
- Day 5 You're on the right track.

2 week

- Day 6 The cure for boredom is curiosity.
- Day 7 When I do good, I feel good.
- Day 8 it's insane to do the same thing over and over again
- Day 9 there is only one success.
- Day 10 Just let it go.

3 week

- Day 11 Healing comes from taking responsibility.
- Day 12 You should be a good listener if you want to be popular.
- Day 13 The biggest communication problem is not to listen to understand.
- Day 14 Confidence is contagious.
- Day 15 you never regret being kind.

4 week

Day 16 In the middle of every difficulty lies opportunity.
Day 17 Giving up is what makes it permanent.
Day 18 You can do anything you want as long as you stick to it long enough.
Day 19 We are refined like gold with every adversity endured.
Day 20 With patient persistence, you will conquer any situation.

5 week

Day 21 the tragedy of life lies in having no goals to reach.
Day 22 If you want something you've never had, then you've got to do something you've never done.
Day 23 you have lots of ideas,
Day 24 you must lose your fear of being wrong.
Day 25 Are you sure you have no dream?

6 week

Day 26 Past, present and future are closely connected.
Day 27 If you want to be happy, give up the past.
Day 28 but it enlarges your future.
Day 29 Life is not measured by its length, but by its depth.
Day 30 be happy with what you have.

7 week

Day 31 create yourself.
Day 32 An important key to self-confidence is preparation.
Day 33 When you say you can, you free the creative powers in you.
Day 34 Those who win are those who think they can.
Day 35 Failure is an opportunity to learn again.

8 week

Day 36 Success sits on a mountain of mistakes.
Day 37 Opportunity is always coming to anybody.
Day 38 Fame is vapor, popularity is an accident.
Day 39 Don't be afraid of being hurt.
Day 40 you enjoy your job.

Happy Language 168

手寫正能量英語：一天一句型，翻轉你的人生和外語溝通力

作　　者	／吳石泰
譯　　者	／葛增慧
發 行 人	／簡志忠
出 版 者	／如何出版社有限公司
地　　址	／臺北市南京東路四段50號6樓之1
電　　話	／（02）2579-6600・2579-8800・2570-3939
傳　　真	／（02）2579-0338・2577-3220・2570-3636
副 社 長	／陳秋月
副總編輯	／賴良珠
責任編輯	／賴良珠
校　　對	／柳怡如
美術編輯	／李家宜
行銷企畫	／陳禹伶・林雅雯
印務統籌	／劉鳳剛・高榮祥
監　　印	／高榮祥
排　　版	／莊寶鈴
經 銷 商	／叩應股份有限公司
郵撥帳號	／ 18707239
法律顧問	／圓神出版事業機構法律顧問　蕭雄淋律師
印　　刷	／祥峰印刷廠

2024年12月　初版

BOOK TITLE: 하루 10분 영어 필사 긍정의 한 줄
Copyright© 2016 by Oh Soktae & E*PUBLIC
All rights reserved.
Original Korean edition was published by E*PUBLIC.
Complex Chinese(Mandarin) Translation Copyright©2024 by Solutions Publishing, an imprint of Eurasian Publishing Group.
Complex Chinese(Mandarin) translation rights arranged with E*PUBLIC.
through AnyCraft-HUB Corp., Seoul, Korea & M.J AGENCY.

定價380元　ISBN 978-986-136-720-0

版權所有・翻印必究

◎本書如有缺頁、破損、裝訂錯誤，請寄回本公司調換　　Printed in Taiwan

抄寫是一個強大的學習工具，透過多種感官啓動與高強度積極參與，來提升你的英文學習體驗。

透過抄寫投入額外的努力和時間，你更有可能做到內化這些文章的教導與智慧，並能夠將它們有意義地應用於你的人生中。

——《抄寫英語的奇蹟》

◆ **很喜歡這本書，很想要分享**

圓神書活網線上提供團購優惠，
或洽讀者服務部 02-2579-6600。

◆ **美好生活的提案家，期待為您服務**

圓神書活網 www.Booklife.com.tw
非會員歡迎體驗優惠，會員獨享累計福利！

國家圖書館出版品預行編目資料

手寫正能量英語：一天一句型, 翻轉你的人生和外語溝通力 / 吳石泰著；
葛增慧譯. -- 初版. -- 臺北市：如何出版社，2024.12
272 面；14.8×20.8公分 -- （Happy language；168）
譯自：하루 10분 영어 필사 긍정의 한 줄：작은 습관이 만드는 대단한 영어 실력
ISBN 978-986-136-720-0（平裝）
1.CST：英語 2.CST：會話
805.188   113016144